For ten-year-old me

—Jason

Dedicated to Village Two apartments, where I grew up in Apartment G-1

—Raúl

HOW STUNTBOY
BECAME STUNTBOY

(AND A THING ABOUT A CHAIR)

Roll credits.
    Cue theme music.

No, no, start with the handclaps, *then* the foot stomps. Stomp

LOUDER! LOUDER!

Now bring in the saxophone.

Now, the song.
And a one, and a *two*, and . . .

WeLLLlllLcoMe to
StUNtboyYYyy in the
MeaNNnnNnTIme!

INTRODUCING THE ONE AND
ONLY . . .

This is **STUNTBOY.**
This guy, right here.
HIM.

You can't tell just looking at him, but he's the greatest superhero you've never ever heard of. And the reason you've never ever heard of him is because his superpower is making sure all the other heroes stay super. And safe. Supersafe. And he does it all on the hush. That's right—it's a secret. A secret secret. But now, because of my big mouth, *you* know. So if you see him, don't call him Stuntboy. At least not when his mum, or his dad, or his granny, or any other heroes are around. Because they only know him by his secret identity. By his household name. His human name. But I clearly can't keep secrets (or secret secrets), so I might as well tell you that name, too, which happens to be **the best human name that a superhero can have—**

Portico Reeves.

But in order to understand how he became the greatest superhero you've never ever heard of, you first have to know where it all started—

in a castle.

THE BIGGEST HOUSE

Portico Reeves lives in **the biggest house on the block**. The biggest house in the whole wide neighborhood. Maybe even the biggest house in the whole wide city.

IN THE WHOLE WIDE EVERYWHERE

Don't know if you would consider it a castle or nothin' fancy like that, but to Portico, it sure seems like one. A giant castle of rectangles made from the glassiest glass and the brickiest bricks on Earth.

Okay, so some people call where Portico Reeves lives an apartment building—Skylight Gardens. And that's fine, too. No matter what it's called, Portico feels lucky to live there. And why wouldn't he? Living in an apartment building is the best. It's like living in a television where behind every door is a **new TV show**.

And Portico knows *all* the characters.

Like **Mr. Mister,** who stands outside **apartment 1B** all day long tying and retying and re-retying and re-re-retying his shoes, tighter and tighter each time. He does this because he's scared he'll leave his feet somewhere, and as long as he has on shoes, he knows he's still . . . feeted (which is way better than being de-feeted)!

Or **Frisbee Foster** in **apartment 3G,** who got her nickname from being thrown back and forth by her big sisters when she was a baby.

Or even the kooky characters in Portico's apartment, like his grandma **Gran Gran**, who was so old, her hair had changed colors from black to gray to white to . . . purple!

Oh, and let's not forget about the smarty, arty, purry, furry family cat who's called

A New Name Every Day.

But enough about them. Portico's granny and cat are cool—especially the cat—but the best thing climbing walls and jumping off counters in **apartment 4D** is **Portico** himself.

Only problem is, he also has a terrible case of . . .

THE FRETS

What?

You've never heard of the frets?

You're kidding, right?

The un-sit-stillables?

The worry wiggles?

The bowling ball belly bottoms?

The jumpy grumpies?

(Or the grumpy jumpies, depending on who you ask.)

The hairy scaries, or worse, the VERY hairy scaries?

No?

Maybe it's because your mum probably calls it what Portico's grandma calls it—"anxiety." (That *X* is tricky, ain't it? Might cause some *anxiety*.

Try this: **ang-ZY-uh-tee.**)

Just means there's nervous in the brain that makes nervous in the body. **That's . . . THE FRETS!**

And the only person who ever seems to be able to help Portico get **unnervous** and **de-fret** is the other best person in the building—the one and only, **only and one . . .**

drumroll, **please . . .**

Zola Brawner!

Zola lives one and a half doors down from **Portico**. They're best friends. **Like, best best.** Two fingers on a two-finger hand. Known each other for, let me think . . . 163 days **(163 days?!)**, and declared themselves best friends on day number one, which is all the time you really need to know if someone's your best friend or not.

It all happened after the first day of school. Zola was new, just moved in to Skylight Gardens. She hopped off the bus, and **guess who came chiming** and **sliming up like** the **stinkiest, weenaged snot-bot ever,** who thinks he's *not* the **stinkiest, weenaged snot-bot ever,** just because he got an earring he swears he put in his ear all by himself and didn't even cry—**Herbert Singletary the Worst.** (Yes, that's his real name.)

When Herbert Singletary the Worst saw Zola, he couldn't help himself.

This is NOT what he was going to say.

But before he could get out whatever mean joke he *was* going to say, Portico came jumping off the bus. And once Herbert Singletary the Worst saw **Portico**, his face went from regular **mean**, to jokey-jaw, teasy-teeth, haha-head mean. The worst.

"Look who it is. Snortico Sneeze," Herbert said instead.

Portico had shown her how to get to the bus stop earlier that morning, and now he was going to show her how to get back home.

It's fine? So, you good with your dad smelling like a ham-and-poop sandwich?

You saying you don't mind the smell of toe jam and ear back?

That one threw Portico for a loop. He'd never actually smelled the back of his ear. Toe jam, well, that's a different story.

Herbert Singletary the Worst followed Portico and Zola into their apartment building and onto the elevator. "And what about your mum? She still cutting hair?"

"Yeah." Portico looked down at his own feet. His brain started churning and the inside-mixup got going. His heart dropped to where his stomach was. And his stomach jumped up to his heart space, which meant his stomach started beating and his heart started growling. Oh no . . . here come . . .

"Then why yours look like a chewed up **pencil eraser?**" Herbert kept mocking, slapping Portico on the back of the head.

He went on and on, boasting and roasting, all while trailing Portico and Zola down the hall. "With parents like that, who you gonna be when you grow up?" Herbert taunted. "Oh, I know. **Probably . . . n o b o d y!**"

Portico wanted to turn around and tie Herbert Singletary the Worst into the best knot ever. A triangle double-half hitch **you-can't-get-this-knot-out** knot, like the one Mr. Mister showed him how to make for his trainers. But Portico tried fighting back once before, and . . . let's just say it didn't work out so well.

After an eon, Portico finally arrived at 4D, his apartment, and tapped on the door lightly. His grandma was always home.

"**Gran Gran,**" Portico called. His voice, breaky and shaky. "**I'm home. Let me in, please.**" But Gran Gran never came. Portico was pretty sure she was resting her eyes. She was so old and had seen so much—she used to be a nurse and looked at balloons and tubes and squigglies for a thousand years—her

eyes *always* needed rest. Only problem was, whenever she was resting her eyes, her ears seemed to be resting too. And . . . her mouth seemed to snore. Or is that her nose?
Weird.

Luckily—what with Herbert now whispering insults to Portico like sour secrets, and the frets turning Portico's insides into a tower of terrible—Zola's mum opened the door to their apartment, 4E. *Phew!*

"Hey, kids, how was the first day of school?" Mrs. Brawner asked.

"Fine," said Zola.

"Most educational," said Herbert Singletary the Worst, pretending to be Herbert Singletary the Angel, which was NOT a thing. "**See y'all later.**" Herbert grinned as he backed down the hall. Guess there were more mean shenanigans for him to shell out downstairs.

Portico didn't say nothing.

"What's that face, young man?" Mrs. Brawner asked. "It's Portico, right?"

Portico nodded. Knocked on his door again.

"What's wrong, Portico? Nobody there?" asked Mrs. Brawner.

Well, you're welcome to hang out here.

THE HALF DOOR

Remember when I said Zola lived one and *a half* doors down from Portico? Well, between Apartment 4D and Apartment 4E, there was another door.

But not a whole door like Portico's and Zola's. A *half* door. A door that looked like it had been cut down the middle. Neither Portico or Zola knew why there was a door there or what was actually behind it. All Portico and Zola knew was that Herbert Singletary the Worst lived there.

THE BIRTH OF

STUNTBOY

(THE MOMENT YOU'VE ALL
BEEN WAITING FOR)

Once inside, Zola tried to get Portico to calm down.

"You okay?" she asked. The living room was covered
in lawn chairs, which would've been weird if her father
wasn't a lawn chair salesman. But he is. Zola calls them
"yawn chairs," because she thinks it's funny and because
they're perfect for napping. **"Portico, you okay?"**

Portico couldn't answer. **Too much fretting going on.**

Zola frowned, then unfrowned.

"I know what," she said, sitting on one of the chairs. **"Let's meditate."**

"I don't want no medicine," Portico mumbled.

"It's not . . . medicine," Zola said, giving Portico bozo eyes. "Well, it sort of is, but not the drinky kind. My mother taught me." Mrs. Brawner was a breathing teacher. As in she taught people how to breathe so they could remember they were still alive.

Portico sat on the lawn chair next to Zola's.

"Okay, so, first make yourself a pretzel," Zola said.

"You got pretzels?!" A snack might be perfect for de-fretting. Might put his belly back in its belly pocket.

"No, make *yourself* a pretzel." Zola crossed her legs.

Portico did the same.

"Now, close your eyes. Take deep breaths. In through the nose, out through the mouth."

Portico followed every single instruction. His mother would've been proud.

"You like TV shows?" Zola asked suddenly. Even though he had no clue why she was asking this in the middle of meditation'ing, it was the perfect question because Portico happened to love TV shows. I mean, doesn't everyone? TV shows were the best things ever invented. Better than video games. Better than candy. Better than drawing (but drawing's pretty cool). And definitely better than books.

"I love TV shows!" he said. "They the best things ever invented. Better than video games. Better than candy. Better than drawing, but drawing's pretty cool. And definitely better than—"

"Shhhhh! Close your eyes."

"How you know my eyes open if your eyes ain't open?" he asked.

"I can hear that they open."

Wait, what? Was he blinking too loud?

Either way, he closed his eyes again.

"What's your favorite kind of TV show?" Zola asked.

This was easy. **Easy, easy.** Portico loved all kinds of TV shows, but he loved one kind of TV show best.

"Superhero shows."

"**Mine too!** I wanna write my own when I grow up."

"How many you seen?"

"I don't know, a lot."

"I seen a lot times infinity."

"Focus, Portico," Zola said. "So my mother says life is just a TV show, and we're all characters in it. So, what if we imagine this is a superhero show and both of us get to pick one superhero to be?"

"Any superhero?"

"Any superhero."

Portico couldn't think of anyone. I mean, his father came to mind, hanging off the back of the rubbish truck, slinging gross things into the metal mouth of his pet monster. He thought about his mum, too. Using those clippers like weapons. But how he could he pick between the two? He even thought about Gran Gran. I mean, she'd memorised every weird thing in the body and *actually* saved lives when she was a nurse. To Portico, they were all heroes . . . but not *super*heroes. **Not high-sky-flying, stronger than bodybuilders, buildings, boulders, and bad guys, kind of superheroes.** He couldn't imagine himself as none of those.

"I don't know," he said, stumped. **"Who would *you* be?"**

And without hesitation, Zola replied, **"I'd be Mater—from**

SUPER SPACE WARRIORS:"

She took a deep breath. In through the nose, out through the mouth. "So, that's me. **You think of anybody, yet?**"

"Oh, uh, wow . . . ummm . . ." Portico thought frantically (definitely not meditation'ing-ly). "I mean, I guess all I can really see me being is a . . . Super Space Warrior too."

"Ain't no Super Space Warrior Two."

"No, I mean, me too. Like, **I'm a Super Space Warrior, _too_**. And plus, there's two of them. **They're twins. Mater and Pater.** I can be Pater."

"We **both** can't play Super Space Warriors, Portico," Zola said. "Also, there are loads of superheroes to choose from."

29

"Okay, okay. But maybe . . . maybe you can be a Super Space Warrior doing, like, all the talking and the acting stuff. And I can be a Super Space Warrior doing the **fighting and flipping stuff.**"

"You mean like . . . a . . . what you call the people who do the dangerous things?"

"A dummy?"
                "No."
                        "A boy?"

"Please. I can do dangerous stuff too. I'm just too smart to."

"Right. So a dummy."

"You not a dummy! It's something else. A . . . a . . ."
        Zola opened her eyes.
                "A stuntman boy?"

Portico opened his eyes too.

"*Yeah*, a stuntman boy. That way *you* can be the hero but don't gotta get hurt."

Portico had never thought about being a stuntman boy before, but now, after meditation'ing, he couldn't see a reason to be anything else. "But that ain't really **a superhero.**"

"It could be.

You could be . . .

STUNTBOY!"

Portico thought about it for half a second.

"I like it. How 'bout Stuntboy the Stunty McStuntster? Too much? You're right. Just . . . Stuntboy. **That's me.**"

"**That's you,**" Zola confirmed. "So what's your superpower, Stuntboy?"

"Keeping other superheroes safe, so *they* can save the world!"

"Hmm. I like that. Kinda like you did with that Herbert kid—" Zola started, but Portico cut her off.

"The Worst."

"Yeah! Like . . . like . . . he *really* wanted to pick on *me*, but then he saw you, and you basically ended up doing all my . . .
                                              stunts."

"Wait, yo . . . you RIGHT!" Portico couldn't believe it. He'd been Stuntboy before he even *knew* he was Stuntboy! **Destiny, folks.** That's what you call this. Destiny.
"Wow, that breathing thing with the pretzel, or whatever, is good," Portico said.

"I told you. It's all in the inhale-exhale. I think. My mum be telling people to breathe in from their feet all the way up to the tops of their heads." Portico didn't get it. And honestly, neither did Zola. So they laughed about how that was impossible because there's "no noses on your toeses."

And then they watched an episode of *Super Space Warriors*.

Zola repeated all the words. Portico threw himself into walls.

And that's how they became **best friends on day number one.**

Oh, and also
how Stuntboy was born.

IN CASE YOU WERE WONDERING

Homework isn't dangerous, and doesn't require stunts.
Nice try.

Stunts have amazing names. At least Stuntboy's do. He learned
how to name stuff from his grandma. When he was little, Gran
Gran would show him a picture of the inside of a human body.
Not like the real inside, but a drawing. Nurse stuff. And she'd
explain each inside-thing by giving it a funnier name.

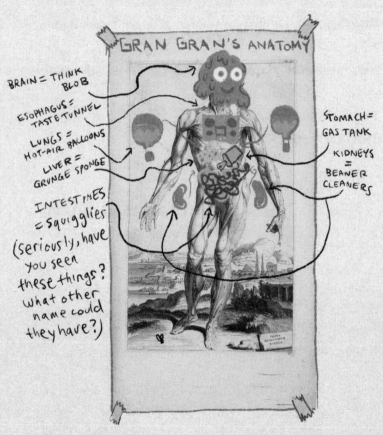

GRAN GRAN'S ANATOMY

BRAIN = THINK BLOB

ESOPHAGUS = TASTE TUNNEL

LUNGS = HOT-AIR BALLOONS

LIVER = GRUNGE SPONGE

INTESTINES = Squigglies
(seriously, have you seen these things? what other name could they have?)

STOMACH = GAS TANK

KIDNEYS = BEANER CLEANERS

So when Portico started coming up with his special stunts,
he gave them all even special-er names.

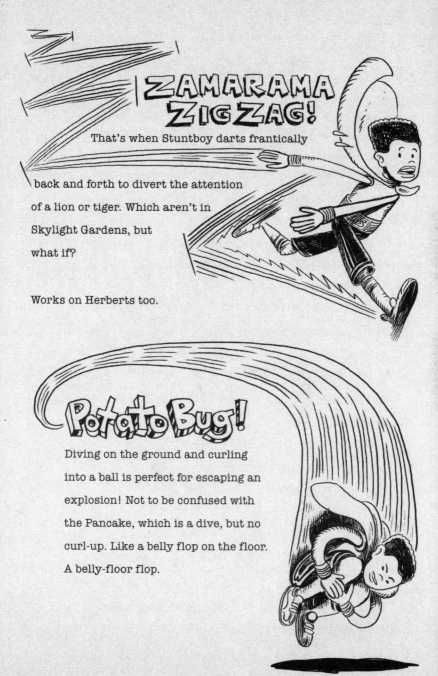

ZAMARAMA ZIGZAG!

That's when Stuntboy darts frantically back and forth to divert the attention of a lion or tiger. Which aren't in Skylight Gardens, but what if?

Works on Herberts too.

Potato Bug!

Diving on the ground and curling into a ball is perfect for escaping an explosion! Not to be confused with the Pancake, which is a dive, but no curl-up. Like a belly flop on the floor. A belly-floor flop.

THE PLASTER BLASTER!

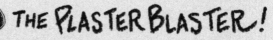

This used to be called the Boomerang Wall Bounce, which is when he jumps into a wall and uses his foot to spring off it. Portico's mother doesn't like it when he does this because she doesn't think feet belong on walls. But, for Stuntboy, anything to save the day. Honestly, he's never actually used this one. But he practices it a lot. Along with the Kick Ball, the Truck Wheel, the Untied Glide, the Didn't Even See You Standing There, and many more, all of which he came up with on his very first day as Stuntboy.

(If Gran Gran wasn't asleep—and if the whole Stuntboy thing wasn't a secret—she would've been proud.)

PLASTER

BLASTER

FAST-FORWARD 3,768 HOURS,

which equals: **113 days** of school, which means **113 days** of the bus ride home, which means **113 days** of Herbert Singletary the Worst waiting there for Portico, so he could be ... **the Worst, which means 113 days** of the Zamarama Zigzag, which means **113 days** of Gran Gran resting her eyes through Portico's knocking on the door, which means **113 days** of yawn chair meditations, which— if you count weekends—means **157 days** of watching TV together (all kinds, but mainly *SSW!*), which means **157 days** of stunt inspiration and practice, which means **157 times** Portico saved people. Well, Zola. He saved her from Herbert, but also things she couldn't see, like the time Sara Moss broke wind on the school bus, and Stuntboy stood in front of her and inhaled it all through his nose to stop Zola or anyone else from having to smell it. Sara literally broke wind. As in she forreal broke the wind. Made the bus hot. Made Stuntboy break out in a sweat. Honestly, that one almost took him out. He named that stunt

the Never Again.

Or like the time he saw Mr. Chico in the stairwell. The elevators were broken, so Mr. Chico had to take the stairs, but he was a **little wobbly**. Mr. Chico was always a little wobbly.

"You okay, Mr. Chico?" Portico asked.

"Yeah, just trying to get my . . . my . . ." and before he could say the word "balance," Portico—I mean, Stuntboy— showed up and tumbled down the steps for him.

And when Stuntboy looked up from the bottom of the stairs,

there Mr. Chico was, still at the top. He looked frazzled, but guess what? He hadn't fallen! Know why? Because Stuntboy fell for him.

COMMERCIAL BREAK:
This commercial is being brought to you by

HOW TO ROLL DOWN STEPS SAFELY

(or HOW TO DO THE CHICO STEP STUMBLE)

Step 1. Well, the point is to kind of miss step one, right?

Step 2. Wear a helmet, shoulder pads, knee pads, elbow pads, a neck pad, a back pad, and a mouthpiece, and most importantly, DON'T ROLL DOWN STEPS!

Just . . . pretend to.

Remember, Stuntboy is a professional superhero.

Now back to your regularly scheduled program.

CHICKEN AND GRAVY MEANS GOOD NEWS

So anyway, **157 days** later, school was off and summer was on. One night, after a dinner of smothered chicken, peas, and carrots—Portico's favorite, minus the peas and carrots, which he gave to the cat (*yuck*)—his mum and dad broke the news.

"We're moving," his mother said.

Portico dropped his fork and choked on a
pea he'd never even put in his mouth.

"But we're not really going nowhere. Just moving to an
apartment downstairs. Apartment 3C," his father said.

"And we're gonna take an apartment upstairs. Apartment 5F,"
his mother said. She pointed up. "It won't be today or tomorrow,
but soon."

Portico didn't know what to say. His father grabbed his hand. "We
want you to know **we love you** and nothing will change, but we—"

"What you mean nothing will change? Of course

things will change," Portico said. He thought about Herbert Singletary the Worst and the terrible things he'd said about Portico's parents just that morning. About how his dad smelled like hippopotamus butt and his mum cut hair with a plastic spoon. But this . . . this . . .

"This is GREAT news! *Everything* will change because now we have TWO apartments!" Portico cheered. "That's TWO new places for me and Zola to watch TV, and TWO new places for me to practice my stunts!" Portico jumped up from the table, excitement all over his face like a new kind of gravy.

"Okaaay . . . ," his mother said. She looked at Portico's dad, and they both shrugged.

A DIFFERENT TUNE FOR A MUSICAL CHAIR

A few days after that, after telling Zola the big news, after the two of them went on tours of the third floor and fifth floor (which were both lovely floors), Portico was in the middle of stunt training when he heard a bunch of noise in the living room. And when he went to see what was going on, he saw his parents doing something he'd never seen them do: **yelling. At each other. Fighting over . . . a chair.** And not like a golden throne that would usually be found in a castle. But fighting

over an old fold-up chair that sat in the corner with never no butts on it. **Not even the cat's butt.**

"The chair goes upstairs with me!" Portico's mum shouted.

"No, it doesn't. It's just as much mine as it is yours!" his father shouted back.

The thing about this chair was that even though it wasn't fancy, it also wasn't just any fold-up chair like the ones on the pavement where the men like Mr. Chico play cards. Portico's parents had had this chair since they'd met, which was a trizillion gillion years ago when they were Portico's age.

It was Sports Day, and little Mrs. Reeves, well, back then she was Apple-Head Sasha, and Mr. Reeves who was Peanut-Head Marvin, were all jazzed up to compete in relay races, dance contests, tugs-o-wars, and all kinds of other outside games. But it rained. So they ended up playing one of the greatest inside games of all time, besides, of course, duck-duck-goose: **musical chairs.**

The teachers organized the fold-up chairs into a cluster and turned on the music. All the Year 5's at Greenfield Elementary, in the class of a long long long time ago, started walking around the chairs. Some kids walked slowly, some danced, and as long as that music played they kept moving. And when it stopped . . . **they SAT!**

The first few rounds were pretty silly. Kids were everywhere—on the ground, under the seats, on each other's laps. But eventually there were less chairs and less kids, and less chairs and less kids, until the final chair, and the final two kids. **Sasha and Marvin.**

The music played.
They circled the chair.
The music played.
They circled the chair.
The music.
The chair.
Circle.
Circle.
C i r c l e . . . SIT!

And Sasha and Marvin both plopped down on the chair. Half and half. Perfect split. There was no way to choose a winner, so they both won. And the prize was . . . you guessed it, **the chair!**

I know, that's a terrible prize. But like I said, this was a long, long time ago. The good prizes hadn't been invented yet.

THE MEANTIME

"What's going on?" Portico now asked, his parents still arguing over the musical chair. Remember how I talked about the letter *X* causing anxiety? Well, to Portico, his parents had basically become screaming *X*s. But once they saw Portico standing there, **they stopped.**

"Oh, Portico. **Nothing's going on,**" his mother said. "We're just having a disagreement, **that's all.**"

"Well, maybe you need to make yourselves pretzels and meditate," Portico suggested. "Or you could try breathing through your toes."

"No . . . no," his father said, clearly thrown off. "We'll figure it out. Don't worry about us."

"As a matter of fact, in the meantime, why don't you go see what Zola is up to," his mum added.

Portico took ten steps to Zola's—sneaking past the half door, of course—and knocked.

"Hey, Portico," Mrs. Brawner said, opening the door with a smile. "Zola's in the courtyard." So to the stairwell Portico went. To him, the lift was for up and the stairs were for down, for leaping whole flights and rail-riding others until he got to the ground floor.

The courtyard wasn't a court, or a yard, really. Just an open space between the apartment buildings. A community garden (that grows peas and carrots). A fountain with no water in it. A good place for rollerskating, if that's your thing.

Zola was there, just like her mother said, kicked back on a yawn chair.

"They fighting over a chair, and when I asked them what was going on, they told me they were in the mean time. I never seen them in the mean time before."

"Was it mean?"

"Oh, it was *mean*," Portico said. "I even thought about getting A New Name Every Day out of there. **That's how mean it was.**"

"Sheesh. Tell me, like . . . what is happening?"

"I just did."

"No, I mean, *tell me*, tell me. Because it got your frets on freak-out!"

Portico broke it all down for her. The words. Pulling the chair back and forth. The way their faces looked like paper balls. He tried to give as much detail as possible.

"And then they told me to leave . . .
                              in the mean time."

Zola nodded one second, shook her head the next.

"You know what this sounds like?

Like Episode **2** of

SUPER SPACE
WARRIORS

when Mater and Pater find out they the only people on Earth who can protect the sun from burning out, because—"

"If the sun burns out, then Earth will die."

"Right—and on this episode, they find out about the Irators, the aliens that are basically planning on putting out the sun, right?

So, Mater and Pater decide instead of waiting for the Irators to come attack, they're just gonna build a spaceship."

"The *Sunjet!*"

"Right, the *Sunjet*. And they were gonna use it to go to space before the Irators even tried to attack the sun.

But when they got in the *Sunjet*—"

"They both grabbed the steering wheel, right?"

"Yeah, because they both felt like they deserved to fly the *Sunjet*."

"And . . . didn't they like . . . break it?"

"Yep! They *broke* the steering wheel! Then a whole bunch of wires started doing electrical stuff, sparking and sizzling and all that. And all of a sudden—"

Portico's eyes got big. Like, BIG. The TV in Portico's brain turned on. "So . . . you telling me that's what's happening with my parents?"

"No, I'm just saying, based on what you've told me, it reminds me of that episode . . ."

But Portico had already stopped listening. Because his taste tunnel had switched places with his gas tank, his stomach now coughing. The inside-mixup. The frets! The frets!

"My parents . . . they in danger. They might break something. A steering wheel. How they gonna turn without a steering wheel?"

"I thought they were arguing about a chair—"

"What if they . . . explode!" He jumped up.

"Wait, what?"

"My dad ain't fast enough to outrun fire!"

"No, wait . . ."

"Nope, gotta go, Zola. **Anything could happen.** *Anything.* **Especially in the mean time!**"

"Portico, I think maybe you—"

THEY NEED ME! THEY NEED... STUNT BOY!

GOING UP

Portico dashed from the courtyard into the building and waited for the lift—or as Portico called it, the elevator— patiently. Well, actually, not so patiently.

"Hi, Ms. Rosedale," Portico said to the older woman who was also being a vator-waiter.

When the doors opened, they both got on. Portico pushed the number four.

Ms. Rosedale, well, she couldn't see a thing, so she pushed EVERY SINGLE OTHER NUMBER. One, two, three, five, six, seven, eight (bingo!), nine, and ten. This made a lot of people vator-waiter haters. But not Portico. Ain't have it in him.

"Who's that?" Ms. Rosedale said, squinting at Portico.

Second floor. Doors open.
Doors close.

"It's me, Portico."

> **"Oh. Hi, son.** How you doing?"

I'm okay. Just gotta go save my parents.

Third floor. Doors open.
Doors close.

"What you say, baby?"

Fourth floor. Doors open.

Herbert Singletary the Worst had just come out of the half-door dungeon and was standing in the way of Portico's apartment like a human hurdle! Ugh! Portico's parents were a few moments away from pretty much blowing up. And Portico, now Stuntboy, had

STUNT TIME

Stuntboy stormed into the apartment and charged into the living room.

"Truck Wheel!" he shouted, rolling into the middle of the floor.

"Floppity-Flip!" he yelled, flipping over the musical chair.

"Pancake!" he howled, landing right (wrong) on his belly. *Oof!* The fall knocked the wind out of him.

He was still working on that one. Either way, once he'd finished rolling, and flipping, and oof-ing, he looked up. His parents stared at him. First, they looked a little concerned. Then they smiled, and it seemed like the mean time had ended. No explosions.

"You okay, Portico?" his mother asked.

"Yeah, son, you cool?" From his father.

"Yeah, yeah. Just . . . just . . . doing my job," he panted, out of breath. "Y'all cool?"

"Yeah, I think so," Portico's father said. He turned to Mrs. Reeves. "You take the chair."

"No, it's fine. You can have it," she said.

"No, it's yours. Go for it."

"It's ours. But I think you should take it."

"No, you take the chair, and I'll take . . . this . . ."

"Ahem." Gran Gran cleared her throat. At least they all

thought it was Gran Gran. But she was in the middle of resting her eyes. And it wasn't Portico, who now sat next to her on the sofa with the remote pointing at the TV.

And it couldn't have been **A New Name Every Day.**

Or could it?

Episode 2

LAWN CHAIRS, PICTURE FRAMES, AND BULLY BUGS

Roll credits.
Cue theme music.

No, not *that* theme music. This is the episode where we bring in the choir to make music with their mouths. Yes, the children's choir *and* the oldie choir. Squeaks and howls are what we're looking for here. Got it? Squeaks and howls.

Good, good.

Now, the song. What's that? Yes, I know it's going to be hard for the choir to make music with their mouths and sing at the same time, but I've seen Portico smack on his food and talk at the same time, so I know it's possible.

And a one,
   and a two, and a . . .

WeLLLllllcoMe to STUNtboyYYyy in the MeaNNnnNnTIme!

SUPER-DUPER STUPERVILLAIN

So now you know **Stuntboy.**

But did you know, before he even became the greatest superhero you've never ... well ... you just heard of, he'd already had a supervillain? That's right. And that supervillain's name is ...

Duh, duh,
duhhhhhhhhhhhh.

But before Herbert Singletary the Worst was **Herbert Singletary the Worst**, he was just Herbert Singletary, the new kid in the building.

And before he was the new kid in the building, he was just **Li'l Herby**. That's what his mama calls him. Can you believe that? **Li'l Herby!**

Herbert—I mean, *Li'l Herby*—grew up in a house somewhere where houses are. I'm not sure, but I bet Herby's house had a few windows, maybe two bathrooms. And maybe in the backyard there was just a whole bunch of green, grassy nothing.

I don't know if any of this is really how Li'l Herby's house was, wherever his house was, which is wherever houses are. But what *is* true is Herby's mother, Mrs. Singletary the Mum, married a man who lived in Skylight Gardens. And it's a good thing she did, because Herby and his mother got to upgrade from their house to this castle.

(But this is another secret. Portico doesn't know this yet.)

WHEN PORTICO MET LI'L HERBY

When Portico met Li'l Herby, he was sitting on a bench outside the building. Portico had seen him a few times before—in the elevator or in the lobby—and every time he saw him, Li'l Herby looked sad. Portico, with his arm elbow-deep in a bag of crisps, sat next to him.

"Want some?"

"..."

"Hey, you want some of these barbecue crisps?
They delicious. Even my cat likes 'em."

". . ."

"You know what's weird about barbecue crisps? They don't
taste like nothing I ever had at a barbecue. Not even
potato salad, which seems like it would be easy because
crisps are potatoes. Ain't that strange?"

". . ."

"So, you new around here?"

"Don't matter. I ain't staying."

"What? Why wouldn't you want to stay here? I mean, I don't
know where you from, but this . . . all *this*, is a castle."

"Is that what you think?"

"Yep."

"You really think this
place is a castle?"

"Yep."

Li'l Herby started laughing, and Portico didn't understand why
he was laughing but figured it was okay because laughing was

better than crying. But then Li'l Herby started crying, and Portico figured that was okay too, because sometimes you cry when you laugh real hard. But then Li'l Herby's mother called for him from one of the many castle windows.

"Li'l Herby!" she shouted. Li'l Herby twisted his face all up like he was trying to get his eyes to suck the tears back in. "Li'l Herby, you better get in this house!"

Portico reached out to shake Herby's hand. "I'm Portico. Welcome to the castle, Li'l Herby."

But Li'l Herby didn't shake Portico's hand, or give him a five, or nothing like that. Instead, he pushed Portico off the bench and onto the ground. Snatched the bag of crisps from him.

My name is Herbert Singletary. If you ever call me Li'l Herby again, you're gonna pay for it.

Pay for what? I don't think I should have to pay nothin' to get knocked on the ground, or get my crisps ate. Plus, I don't have no money, anyway.

Herbert glared at Portico with mean eyebrows and stormed off.

Portico got the message. No more Li'l Herby. Instead, Portico called him **Herbert Singletary the Sad**. Then, after a few more push-downs and put-downs (and those eyebrows), Portico started calling him:

HERBERT SINGLETARY THE WORST.

(Portico also switched to salt & vinegar crisps because they taste like salt . . . and vinegar. You ever had them? A better question is:)

HAVE YOU EVER SOLD A LAWN CHAIR?

Okay, so in case you haven't figured it out yet, Herbert ain't the best. Far from it. But Zola . . . **well, she's amazing.** And her mum's amazing. Guess who else is amazing? Her dad. Mr. Brawner. He sold lawn chairs (I know I told you that already but it's so cool I had to say it again). On Day 169 of Portico and Zola's best best friendship, Mr. Brawner interrupted them as they were watching TV. Well, they weren't just watching TV. Portico was drawing what was on the screen (told you drawing is cool), which was hard because what was on the screen kept moving. And Zola was rewriting every line of the show in the way she thought it really should go. Drawing and writing . . . **and watching TV.**

"Dad, this the best part!" Zola shrieked, trying to see around her father.

"Plus, I'm almost done with the *Sunjet*!" Portico added, in the middle of drawing one of the wings.

"I know, I know, but I have a question for you two lawn chariots," Zola's father said. He loved lawn chair jokes. Especially corny ones. Sometimes he called Zola and her mum his sweet lawn cherries. As in, *chair*-ies. As in, if you knew him, **you'd love this guy.**

Portico and Zola sat up.

"How would y'all like to come on a job with me?"

"What you mean?" Zola asked, sitting up *more*.

"I mean, come with me to sell a lawn chair."

Portico looked at Zola; Zola at Portico.

"YES!" they both said, instantly scrambling for their shoes.

Mr. Brawner went over to one of his many lawn chairs and folded it in half.

"Who you selling it to?" Portico asked, double knotting. "Hopefully my mum and dad. But we're going to need two. One for each of our apartments."

"Y'all got two apartments?" Mr. Brawner asked, pausing.

"We will soon," Portico said. "They been organising stuff. The musical chair goes in this pile. The not-musical ironing board goes in that pile. You know . . . sharing." He shrugged.

"Well . . . congratulations," Mr. Brawner said. "But this beauty is going to Ms. Majesty Morris. Up on the tenth floor." Mr. Brawner lifted the chair, but Portico stopped him.

"I got it! I got it!" he said.

"Careful. It's pretty heavy, kid."

"Yeah, but I don't want you to hurt yourself," Portico said.
"I can do it." This was just another day as Stuntboy, doing
his job so the real heroes stay safe. But when Portico tried
to lift it, he realized his muscles were probably a little tired
from all the . . . drawing.

Zola grabbed the other side. "We can do it together," she said.

Mr. Brawner moseyed down the hall, Portico and Zola panting
and gasping, their heads becoming hot-air balloons. Who knew
those things were so heavy?

They shuffled past open doors of some of their castlemates.
Like Mama Gloria, who ain't nobody's mama but acts like
she's *everybody's* mama.

Her apartment door was open because she was cooking
greens, and greens always stink up the place. So instead of

Where y'all going with that chair?

70

it making just *her* apartment smell like veggie funk (which smells like poop), she preferred to make the *whole floor* smell like dog-walker boot bottom (which smells like poop poop). Also, she kept her door open because she was so nosy. If being nosy had anything to do with actual noses, Mama Gloria would have a face full of them. **Just noses, everywhere.**

Portico, Zola, and Mr. Brawner also bumped into the twins, Syl and Byl. The thing about them was that they always claimed to be different-faced, but no one could tell them apart. The other thing about them was that they were the building's dodgeball champions. They were strong enough to make a rubber ball feel like a cannonball.

And on and on, and onto the elevator Portico and Zola went, with Mr. Brawner, the best lawn chair salesman in the building, leading the way.

UP TO THE TENTH FLOOR

The tenth floor was the top floor. The tip-top. Portico had
been up there a bunch of times (see *How to Be a Good
Castlemate*), running in the hall and riding the elevator. But
he'd never been in anyone's apartment up there. He'd never
been able to look out a window and see what life was like
that high off the ground. What the neighbourhood looked like
from the top of the castle.

But this was his chance.

They step-by-stepped all the way to the end of the hall.

"This is it," Mr. Brawner said, tapping on the door. It opened,
and there was Ms. Majesty Morris, who always looked cool
because of her eyes. Well, her eye *makeup*. She would paint
it on so that it looked like wings. Or like she was a cat. Or that
her eyes were cats with wings. **It's hard to explain,**
but . . . the way she painted makeup around her eyes made her
look like she was a costume away from being a superhero, too.
Like she'd forgotten to hide her secret identity as the lady who
lives on the top floor and orders lawn chairs.

"Come on in," she said, moving aside so Portico and Zola could shimmy the chair through the doorway. Once all the way in, Mr. Brawner set the chair up in the middle of Ms. Morris's living room.

"Y'all have a seat on the sofa," he said to Portico and Zola. Just then, Portico had the urge to bust a stunt. Right there, high in the sky. Maybe a Spinnablam, which is when he'd spin until dizzy, then fall out, a move usually seen on funny TV shows. But he didn't. Because if his mother found out he'd Spinnablammed in a stranger's house . . . *duh duh duhhhhhh.*

So he took a stunt-free seat on the sofa. But that seat on the sofa wasn't just a seat on the sofa—it was a seat with a view of the world. Portico looked out the window at all the big things that suddenly seemed like small things. The trees had shrunk. The cars and buses. The snack truck. The people.

"There goes Herbert Singletary the Worst," Portico said. Zola looked down at Herbert, then kissed her teeth.

"Ain't so big from up here," she said. He also wasn't so big from down there.

"Nope, he definitely ain't," Portico said, watching him

hang outside the front of the building, he and his weenaged friends, teeny-tiny like little ants.

"Y'all ready to see magic?" Mr. Brawner asked. Portico and Zola focused on him. The yawn chair was set up and ready to be yawned on. "Here's how you sell a lawn chair."

HOW TO SELL A LAWN CHAIR

Lay on it and pretend to fall asleep. And when the person who is supposed to be buying it gets weirded out about you falling asleep in their living room, open your eyes and say:

"Who needs a lawn **when you can have a yawn**."

Yeah, it's cheesy. But it works. At least it did for Mr. Brawner because Ms. Morris laughed (and snorted) and more importantly, paid.

And the best part about her paying was that then Mr. Brawner invited Portico and Zola to the snack truck outside to get crisps.

"I'll meet y'all out there," Portico said. "I just wanna quick tell my folks about what life is like on the top floor."

So Portico practiced his newest stunt—he'd created it

just moments before, inspired by Mr. Brawner—called the Lawn Chair, which meant he laid on the stairs (because he always took the steps down), and instead of doing the Chico Step Stumble and *rolling* down, Portico *slid* down. Flight after flight after flight after flight after flight after flight. To the fourth floor. Then he broke into a sprint down the hall because he could already hear them.

His parents, arguing inside.

Then he was inside the arguing.

And it was like stepping into static. The kind of static people get on walkie-talkies, when they have to keep saying, *You're breaking up. You're breaking up.*

There they were. His mother and father, two standing statics, this time shouting at each other about—you won't believe it—a picture frame. Not a picture. Just the frame. A piece of wood in the shape of a rectangle. "I don't know why you're fighting me on this. It's my frame. You know it's mine!" Portico's mother shouted, tugging the frame toward her.

"But I made it. These hands made it," said his father, tugging it back.

"But you gave it to me." Tug.

"No, I gave it to you to put a *picture* in, which you never did." Tug.

"Because it's ugly."

"Then why do you want it so bad?"

"Because it's mine. You gave it to me!" Tug, tug, tug.

And then, finally, they noticed Portico standing there with all the excitement of the tenth floor draining out of him.

"What's going on?" Portico asked.
 "Nothing, nothing," his father said.
  "Yeah, nothing," his mother said.

"Sure sounds like something to me," Gran Gran said in the two seconds she was awake.

"We're . . . just having a disagreement about this picture frame," Portico's mother added.

"Well," Portico said, "if you took a picture of what I just saw up on the tenth floor, you wouldn't even *need* a frame."

"You were on the tenth floor?" she asked.

"Yep. Helped Mr. Brawner sell a lawn chair." Portico shrugged. "Now Zola and him are at the snack truck."

"That's cool, but your father and I need to finish this conversation. So, in the meantime, why don't you go get a snack too."

The mean time. Again.

When Portico got outside, Zola was peeling apart an ice cream sandwich, and her father was munching on pumpkin seeds.

"You want some punkin seeds?" he asked, offering Portico the bag, but Portico shook his head.

"You want a bite of my ice cream sandwich?" Zola asked, but again, Portico shook his head.

"Well, what you want, then?" Mr. Brawner asked. **"I gotta pay you for all your hard work."**

"Just some salt and vinegar crisps, please," Portico said.

After Mr. Brawner bought him the crisps, he got into a conversation with Mr. Mister about the best shoestrings he'd ever had. And while those two oldies shared stories about how to keep your shoes tight tight **(TIGHT!)**, Portico and Zola sat on the bus stop bench, snacking away.

"You know what's weird about salt and vinegar crisps?" Portico mumbled, finally saying something.

"What?"

"Vinegar is salty already. So it's basically, salt and more salt crisps." The bitterness made him pucker his lips, kiss the air.

"That's what's making *you* salty?" Zola asked.

"Nah. My parents are the salty ones. They in the mean time again. Now they fighting over a picture frame. Never even had no picture in it. I was gonna put the one I was drawing today in it, you know? The *Sunjet*. Finally fill it with something good."

Zola thought it all over before offering some advice.

"Know what that all reminds me of?"

"What?"

"That episode of **SUPERSPACEWARRIORS** —I think it's **Episode 22**—where Mater and Pater are fighting over the portal necklace, trying to see who gonna put their head through it first. Remember that?"

"Yeah, and whoever put it on zaps back to the past."

"Not just go back. They could mess with history, which could change the present.

Which is why Mater and Pater both wanted to go back back back,

so they could make more sun protectors like them to help fight off the Irators.

But instead of talking about it or making a plan, they just fought over the portal necklace because they both wanted credit, when really they were both already heroes."

"Yeah, 'cept they couldn't really *be* heroes because they were so worried about changing the past that they ain't paying attention to the fact that Irators were attacking the sun."

"I know! They were stealing fire and light from it, while the Super Space Warriors were fighting and fighting and fighting over the portal necklace, pulling and pulling and pulling on it, until . . ."

Zola popped the top cookie of her melting ice cream sandwich into her mouth. But Portico's eyes got big like two crisps.

His brain started buzzing. His insides started piling and mixing up. His squiggles felt like they were wrapping around his beat box like a boa constrictor. "Oh . . . my . . ."

"What?"

"My parents are gonna destroy the past? They're gonna break the portal, aren't they?"

"No, wait. That's not what I'm saying. That's on TV."

"Right. But still . . . I mean, they're on TV. This is TV. Your mum said so!"

"This is not—"

"And I have to stop them!"

"Wait—Portico!" But it was too late. He'd already run off.

"Porticooooooooooooo!"

FRAME FLAME (MADE OF POTATO CHIP CRUMBS)
TO THE RESCUE

As Portico ran back toward the building,
he tried to avoid Herbert Singletary the Worst,
who was still hanging outside with his friends.
They were ants a little while ago, but now they were
different bugs. **Bigger bugs.** **Meaner bugs.**
Portico tried to run past them, when Herbert stuck his
leg out and **tripped him**. Portico fell hard, tumbled,
rolled, but Herbert had no idea that Portico had already
become Stuntboy. So to hit the ground was nothing but an
opportunity to pop back up and keep running. A weird
version of the Truck Wheel stunt.

And that's what Portico did.
(Didn't even drop his crisps. That boy is *good!*)

TRIP

He ran into the lobby, to the elevator. Hit the up button.
> Waited.
>> Waited.
>>> Waited.

(Maybe we should play some music here. Something jazzy. Something that says, *Waiting a long time*.)

Eventually, when the elevator came, everyone in it was getting out of it. So many people that he couldn't make his way inside in time and missed it. Hit the button again.
> Waited.
>> Waited.

Doors opened. He got on, pushed the four button, and on the way up, he practiced **the Plaster Blaster,** just in case.

But he should've been practicing the Didn't Even See You Standing There, because when Stuntboy got to his apartment, he burst through the door to find his parents . . . standing there. His mother shaking her head. His father holding the picture frame, which to Stuntboy was all the reason he needed to go **with Option C.**

"Spilled Milk!" he said, throwing himself onto the floor. He rolled around for a while, slowly (and weirdly) inching toward his father. Then . . . Option W (I didn't even see this one coming). He took a few crisps from the bag and crushed them in his hand.

He blew the chip crumbs into his father's face.

"Gah! What in the world, Portico! It stings! Is that salt and vinegar?!" his father shouted, rubbing his eyes.

He dropped the picture frame.

Portico's mother ran to the kitchen and came back with a damp cloth. She patted Mr. Reeves's eyes until he was able to open them again.

And Gran Gran, suddenly awake again, chuckled, and asked if there were any crisps left.

Episode 3

PARTY ANIMALS WHO TUMBLE DRY

Roll credits.   Cue theme music.

Oh no. Not the same music as the last episode. This episode is festive! It's a party! So how about some noisemakers that sound like screaming cats . . . **or not.**

Now the song,
   which, by the way,
      sounds like screaming kids
who sound like screaming cats.

And a one,
   and a two,
      and a . . .

WelllllllcoMe to
StUNtboyYYyy in the
MeaNNnnNnTIme!

got
Food?

ZOLA GOT A BIRTHDAY

This is . . . well, you know who this is. Or at least who he usually is. But today, Portico Reeves is *not* Stuntboy. He's Portico Reeves, best friend of Zola Brawner, who, 174 days into their best best friendship, has a birthday. And you know what comes with a birthday? **A BIRTHDAY PARTY!**

And who better to help plan a birthday party than your best best, especially when your best best is the one and only **Portico Reeves**.

COMMERCIAL BREAK: This commercial is brought to you by

HOW TO PLAN A BIRTHDAY PARTY

1. Save all your breath because you're going to have to blow up at least a million balloons. Maybe two million. But just so you know, anything over twenty is technically all the decoration you need.

2. Make sure there's cake and ice cream. If you can, get the birthday person's face on the cake. Not necessary, but a nice touch. Also, make sure the ice cream is the kind that's called that funny name. Need-No-Polishin' or Knee-No-Pollen-In. The kind with strawberry, vanilla, and chocolate. This is so you can keep your eye on the weirdo who asks for chocolate ice cream. Also, make sure there's punch. Red punch.

3. Invite (almost) *everybody*. And have a dance contest.

Now back to your regularly scheduled program.

PEOPLE WHO SHOWED UP TO ZOLA'S BIRTHDAY PARTY:

ADRIAN HOLMES, APARTMENT 2G

Superpower: No inside voice, only outside voice. And by outside I mean he speaks loud enough to be heard on the moon. **Dance move:** The sharp shoulder. Basically, imagine someone saying, "I don't know" five thousand times.

ROMAN CARTER, APARTMENT 8A

Superpower: Can and will eat anything. ANYTHING. (Famous for putting relish on his pizza and, if dared, licking doorknobs.) **Dance move:** Well, let's just say we all call it the belly ache. He calls it that too.

JADEN CROWDER, APARTMENT 9F

Superpower: Hair growth. The kid's got more hair than he has head. Like a rockstar. **Dance move:** He calls it the piano, which is weird since it looks more like he's playing a guitar.

YEMI HOLLAND, APARTMENT 1E

Superpower: Fast walking. But not running. NEVER running.

Dance move: Stepping on her own toes. And mine. And, if you came to this party, yours, too.

FRISBEE FOSTER, APARTMENT 3G
Superpower: Flying. It's been a while, but we've all seen it.
Dance move: Corner standing. Growing up with sisters like hers, can't even blame her.

MYA ANGELO, APARTMENT 10A
Superpower: Every grown-up asking her if that's her real name, which doesn't feel like a superpower until you see the way these oldies treat her. Like she famous or something.
Dance move: She don't dance. She just talks to oldies about the music.

STUMP, APARTMENT . . . Wait, does Stump live here?
Superpower: ?? **Dance move:** ???
(Okay, so nobody really knows this kid. But he was at the party.)

And, of course,
PORTICO REEVES, A DOOR AND A HALF DOWN
Superpower: Stunts. **Dance move:** Um . . . stunts.

93

PARTY TIME

Mr. Chico was the DJ. He DJ'ed everybody's parties in the building, and no one really knows how because he always looked like he was a few zeez away from ZZZZZZ. But when it came to playing jams, he was the jammer of all jammers. As soon as the music came blaring through the speakers, Zola, Portico, and the rest of the kids cut loose. Arms and legs   all over the place. Some kids like Adrian flashed big

smiles because dancing is fun, while others like . . . well, like Portico, had a tight face—tight eyes and tight mouth—because his dance moves required concentration. How else could he do a forward roll, then immediately throw himself into a backward roll, and then spring back up to his feet? **Dancing was serious business.**

94

PARTY CRIME

Halfway through the dance contest, which no one was judging because the oldies (and Mya) were too busy talking about boring stuff, there was a knock at the door. And after Mrs. Brawner opened it, she turned to make an announcement.

"Hey, party people, guess who's here?"

"Dad?" Zola called out. He was the last person she was waiting for to arrive.

"Herbert!" Mrs. Brawner squealed.

Herbert Singletary. Half door 4D/E.

Superpower: Normally, stopping superheroes. At this moment, ruining a party. **Dance move:** Well . . . you'll see.

Herbert? Herbert? You mean, Herbert . . . Singletary . . . the Worst? Portico was no longer dancing and had actually joined Frisbee Foster in the corner.

Zola glanced over at her mother, puzzled. Her mother was smiling because she clearly had no idea that Herbert was, in fact, the worst.

"Happy Birthday, Zola," Herbert said, all smarmy.

"Um . . . thanks?" Zola replied. And before anything got weirder than it already was, Mr. Chico got back to the music and the kids got back to dancing.

Even Portico. Slowly. He started with a foot tap, then a finger snap, then a hand clap. And then he did some kind of weird skip over to the floor, before breaking into more of his stunt moves. The Hydrant Hurdle. The Whirly Squirrelly Squat. And Herbert Singletary the Worst, even though he went straight for the chocolate ice cream, seemed to be having fun too.

It was like he was   Herbert Singletary the Not-the-Worst.

Or Herbert Singletary the Party Animal.

Herbert Singletary the Good-Time Guy.

Herbert Singletary the Move Buster.

Herbert Singletary the DJ's Dream.

Herbert Singletary the Getter Alonger.

He was all that.

Until he wasn't.

Until Portico finally found his groove again and attempted his favorite dance stunt:

a walking handstand.

HOW TO DO A WALKING HANDSTAND

or, as Portico calls it,
CRAWLING ON THE CEILING IN AN UPSIDE-DOWN WORLD

1. Become a frog (that is, if you can't become a cat)—not really, but squat like you're becoming a frog.

2. Look behind you to make sure you don't kick nobody in the mouth.

3. Kick your feet up over your head. Become a giraffe. (I know you were just a frog, but there are no limits to what you can become), and pretend your feet are the giraffe's face.

4. And walk. Until you become a turtle. On its back.

OR:

5. Until Herbert Singletary the Worst bumps you . . . "accidentally." (Sure.)

Crash onto a table.

Have that table be covered in cake, ice cream, and punch.

Have that cake, ice cream, and punch fly
E V E R Y W H E R E.

The whole party groaned and howled and made all kinds of other sounds people make when **bad things happen at birthday parties.** And as soon as Portico, all squirmy and freaked out, slowly got up off the floor, the backs of his knees started to itch. His elbows got hot. **And his insides started piling up.** The frets were all up and through him as he looked at Adrian and Roman and Jaden and Yemi and Frisbee (yep, the mess even made it to the corner) and Mya and Stump (???), all covered in sugary pieces of Zola's face. When Portico looked at Zola, her face looked just as smeared. Then he looked at Herbert's face. **On it was a smirk.**

"Hey, Portico," Zola's mother finally spoke up, wiping icing off her forehead with a finger. "It's okay. It was an accident." But before she could even grab a roll of paper towels, Portico, the hero, had become the villain and did what villains often do—he ran away. Well, he didn't run far. He just ran home, and home was only one and a half doors down.

When he shoved his way into the apartment with kick in his belly and punch on his shirt, there in front of him, standing between two growing piles of stuff . . . were his parents. Fighting. *Again.* This time over the table in the living room. The table they called a coffee table, even though it never made coffee. There was never even coffee *on* it. This was the table for magazines, television remotes, Portico's

mother's nighttime tea, and, most often, Gran Gran's feet. **Not coffee.**

Never coffee.

"Listen, I need this table, Marvin. **I don't want to fight you on this,**" Portico's mum said.

"You're already fighting me, Sasha!" his dad said. "**It's not just a table.** You know it's not just a table."

Portico couldn't deal with his parents arguing. **Not today.** Not right then. He was a mess, and had made a mess, and worse, had ruined his best best friend's birthday party, and his parents were too busy arguing about which new apartment this stupid table would live in to even notice.

All Portico knew was that them fighting piled onto the pile that was piled up in him. **All piles, no smiles.** So he ran back out before they even knew he'd come in. As a matter of fact, the only person who noticed him was the cat.

But where could he go? Not back to Zola's, where they were still laughing at him. He couldn't go outside. Not covered in Birthday Party. So he went to the only place he could think of. **The only place that made sense.**

THE LAUNDRY ROOM

In a castle, along with all the windows, doors, and bathrooms, there's also a special room in the basement. Below the first floor. Down down to the zero'th floor. It's a bit noisy, and honestly, **it's kinda weird.**

The laundry room.

On one side there were washing machines lined up like a bunch of submarine portholes. And on the other side, the dryers. Along the back were chairs, and in the middle of the floor, a few tables for folding clothes. But the gem of the room was in the corner, suspended from the ceiling:

a television.

Even better, Portico found he had the place to himself. No one was there doing laundry. Normally, this would be the perfect time to practice his stunts.

To kick and roll and jump and dive. But for the first time in a long time, he wasn't in the mood. Portico grabbed the remote, took a seat next to his sadness, and started clicking.

Finally, some good luck: a *Super Space Warriors* marathon was on!

Portico watched episode after episode as people came and went, putting clothes in the washer, then clothes in the dryer. Folks folding and bagging and dragging clean clothes back upstairs.

After about an hour, Mr. Mister showed up. He came in with a bunch of laces thrown over his shoulder to wash.

"Hey, Portico." Mr. Mister opened a washer door and dumped the laces in like spaghetti. Then he sat a few seats down from Portico and started unlacing the shoes he had on.

"Hey, Mr. Mister."

"Down here washing clothes?"

Mr. Mister asked, but then, realizing Portico's shirt and jeans were covered in Birthday Party, he changed the subject. "Ah. *Super Space Warriors*."

"You watch *Super Space Warriors*?"

"Absolutely not," Mr. Mister said, then winked at Portico. He'd gotten the lace out of his right shoe, and now was working on the left.

"You wash your shoelaces?"

"Of course," Mr. Mister said, finally getting the lace free. He kicked both shoes off and massaged his toes for a moment. The strings had been so tight, they left creases across his feet. Big *Xs*. "Gotta take care of 'em."

"But why you gotta take care of 'em if they hurt you so bad?"

Mr. Mister smiled, then slipped his laceless shoes back on and got up. Uh-oh. Portico knew what was coming. He'd been a superhero for weeks and could see danger before danger knew it was dangerous. He also knew that, as a superhero, you had to do your duty, even when you were down and out. So, Portico knew it was time for an Untied Glide.

COMMERCIAL BREAK: This commercial is brought to you by

HOW TO DO AN UNTIED GLIDE

1. Untie your shoes

2. Do Yemi Holland's dance

3. That's it. (Don't worry. Your knees will feel better in no time.)

Now back to your regularly scheduled program.

As Portico crashed to the ground, Mr. Mister stared.

"Must've tripped on my shoes," Portico said. Mr. Mister shook his head, slipped his feet back out of his shoes, and walked to the washer barefoot.

At least I saved one person today, Portico thought as the oldie put the last set of laces in the washer and added coin and detergent until the machine came alive. Then he turned back to Portico.

"Point is, I take care of these laces because even though they cause me a little pain, they still mine, and I still need 'em."

"I don't get it." Portico rubbed his knees, skinned from the stunt.

"Ask your parents." Mr. Mister sat back down.

"I can't. They in the mean time. They always in the mean time these days."

Mr. Mister squinted. "The mean time?"

Just then, the laundry room door swung open. This time it was Zola.

"Portico, I've been looking everywhere for you!" she said. "I knocked on your door but your folks were ... well, no one came to the door. Then I went out front, but you weren't there. Checked out back, but no you. I even went to the tenth floor. This was the last place I could think of." She paused for a moment. Noticed Mr. Mister. "Oh, hey, Mr. Mister."

"Hello there, Zola." He walked barefoot over to the washer he was using and stared into the glass window as it filled with suds.

Zola plunked down next to Portico.

"What happened to your knees?" she asked.

"Nothing."

"You still sad about the party?"

"Sorry I ruined it."

"You ain't ruin it. It was already kind of ruined anyway, because my dad couldn't make it," Zola said. "Selling lawn chairs is an even busier job than being the president. Besides, we both know what really happened. I can't believe my mother invited Herbert."

"Yeah." Portico glanced up at the TV. Mater and Pater teleported to another planet. "Wish I could do that."

Zola sighed. "What's the mean time about now?"

"A coffee table that don't even make coffee. It don't make nothing, really, except a good storm shelter."

STORM SHELTER TABLE

A few years ago, when Portico was four, maybe five, his parents brought home this table. **They found it** on the pavement outside their building. That happens around here. **Normal.** Sometimes when people are moving, they can't take everything with them so they leave things out front. Other times, when people get new stuff, they put their old stuff out there. I mean, why throw things away, especially when it's as good as this table?

"It's nice," Mrs. Reeves said. And that was all she had to say before Mr. Reeves picked the table up and carried it into the building. He set it down in front of the sofa, and as soon as he did, Gran Gran sat down, opened up a strawberry sweet, and kicked her feet up on it. And her feet stayed there. Along with magazines and diet beverages.

One night, there was a big storm. Thunder and lightning and rain slapping against the windows. The lights flickered and the TV went off. And that's what did it. **You guessed it. The frets.** Scared Portico (and A New Name Every Day) to the point that he (they . . . we) ran and hid under the coffee table.

It was like having an extra sealing, under a ceiling, under a roof.

THUNDERING AND LIGHTNING'ING

"So they fighting over the table?" Zola asked, her ears on Portico but her eyes on the TV.

"Yeah."

"You know what this reminds me of?"

Portico knew.

He knew what she'd say, but he acted like he didn't.

"What?"

"Episode 67 of

SUPER SPACE WARRIORS,

when Mater and Pater were trying to find the Irators' planet, but ended up finding a new planet in the galaxy," Zola said.

"You talking about the square planet?" Portico asked.

"Yep!"

"Yeah, that was kind of a silly episode."

"I know, I know. But remember how for some reason the planet was full of growing things the **Super Space Warriors** could use, like food and stuff like that.

And they were thinking maybe, if something does happen with the sun, they could just move everyone to this new square planet. But then they started arguing about what they were going to name it.

Mater wanted to name it Matercube, and Pater wanted to name it Paterverse."

"And what they didn't know was that the Irators were on the bottom-side of the planet. This whole thing was a trap because they knew Mater and Pater wouldn't be able to stay away from a planet that reminded them of Earth," Portico filled in.

"And right when they'd settled on the name, Sqearth . . ."

AN EXPLOSION OF GREAT MAGNITUDE!

"The Irators destroyed it and almost destroyed them, remember?" Zola asked.

"Um . . . yeah . . . I remember." Portico looked concerned. That concerned look he always gets when his mind is racing at warp speed. When the inside-mixup starts insiding and mixing up. "You think they gonna destroy the table? **Each other?**"

"Who? **Your parents?** Nah, I don't think they'd—"

"Wait, are they the Space Warriors . . . or are they . . . Irators?" Now Portico looked *concerned* concerned.

"**Neither.** They're your parents, and I just meant—"

But it was too late. Portico—I mean, Stuntboy—was already gone.

He sprinted from the laundry room and waited for the elevator. When it finally came, Ms. Rosedale was in it.

"Now, how in the world did I get down here?" she asked.

"Hi, Ms. Rosedale," Portico said, stepping in.

"Who's that?"

"It's Portico."

"Oh, hi baby," she said, and before she could hit every single button, Stuntboy did one of his most underrated stunts—he hit the number eight for her. He calls it the Don't Wait Eight.

(Okay, he doesn't call it that. But he should, right? Either that or the Vator Waiter Eighter. Maybe. I don't know, but if you have suggestions, send them in.)

When they finally made it to the fourth floor, Portico slammed into his apartment. His parents were still arguing, so he dove between them—dove between the two growing tornadoes of family furniture and forget-me-nots, including chairs, ironing boards, an iron, picture frames, and mirrors—and curled up under the table. The Potato Bug.

And Portico's mother and father, who had been storming the apartment for hours, finally, for a moment, **stopped being thunder and lightning**.

Episode 4

SUPER CUT, SUPER . . . WHAT?

Roll credits.
    Cue theme music.

Actually . . . don't. This is an important story, and we should just get to it.

WeLLLlllLcoMe to STUNtboyYYyy in the MeaNNnnNnTIme!!

CUT DAY

CUT DAY

The first Sunday of every month is a special day: Cut Day. As in, haircuts for anyone in Skylight Gardens who wants one. Portico's mum has been doing Cut Day since before Portico was born. Sets up her chair and buzzes, baldys, or fades folks for free.

For Portico, what's fun about Cut Day is getting to see so many of his castlemates come and sit in his mum's chair. It's like a show. But if there's one thing Portico knows about Zola, 181 days into their best best friendship, is that she's pretty bored by this whole thing, so she spends the day roller-skating back and forth from the courtyard to the lobby, where she weaves in and out of the people waiting.

No one stands in line. So, technically, no one could cut the line. Which means, anyone could cut the line. Which is why it was always good that Portico went first.

"I always cut you first—that way the people know *all* customers are welcome," his mother said.

"But I'm your son, so it makes sense that you would be cutting my hair."

"Do you know just how big your head is, boy?" she joked, trimming Portico's high top.

"Same size as yours!" Portico snapped back.

"Nah, you definitely got this watermelon head from your daddy," she said, laughing.

If his mother was a professional haircutter, then that would make him a professional haircuttee. He figured he must be pretty good at it, because by the time his hair was done, people had gathered, inspired to get theirs cut too. At least that's what Portico believed. A sorta-superpower he shared with his mum.

Oldies showed up with chairs to sit on, weenagers like Herbert Singletary the Worst leaned against the wall, watching as Portico's mum perfected Portico's fade. As a final touch she sprayed this stuff on his head that smelled sneezy-sweet—kinda good (kinda), but it made your nose feel itchy. Most importantly, it made your hair look like it was sparkling. Like there were stars in it. A galaxy head. Someting off *Super Space Warriors*.

Mrs. Reeves snatched the smock from around Portico's neck. And he broke into a stunt, a Jumbo Jump. For practice, of course.

HOW TO DO A JUMBO JUMP

1. Find something to jump off. A kerb is recommended. Or in this case, the footrest of a barber chair.

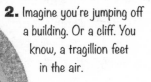

2. Imagine you're jumping off a building. Or a cliff. You know, a tragillion feet in the air.

3. Jump with your whole body. Not just your legs. Swing your arms, bend your back, and make a funny face that looks like you're thinking, WHOAAA, THIS IS HIGHHHH! This is what makes it jumbo.

4. Land on your feet. Or, if you're REALLY good, land on your feet and go into a roll.

Now back to your regularly scheduled program.

"Who's next?" Mrs. Reeves called out. And EVERYONE said, "ME!" "No, I've been keeping watch," she said. "Little Jaden, you up."

Jaden Crowder came stepping up to the chair. His hair was like a swarm of curls above his head.

"What we doing with this today?" Portico's mum asked Jaden's mum.

"Cut it off."
"All of it?"
"All of it."

But Jaden didn't look so sure. As a matter-of-fact he looked pretty nervous. Portico's mum nodded, tied the smock around Jaden's neck, and pulled out a pair of scissors.

Clip. Then *snip.* Then *clip clip. Snip snip.* After cutting some of the longer bits first, it was time to get to work. She hit the switch, and the clippers started to buzz. The crowd fell silent, everyone just watching for what was supposed to happen next. For Jaden's hair to be left in a pile on the floor. But as soon as the clippers touched his head, Jaden was GONE. Portico didn't know where he went. Just knew he went, and he went *fast*. Outta there. With a patch of hair missing.

Portico's mum chuckled. Jaden did this every month, which is why his hair was so long in the first place. She slapped the small trimmings off the seat.

"Next!"

Next up was Romello Mann, a slick-talking pretty boy who everybody called Mello, and who everybody liked but nobody loved. Because he couldn't be trusted. He always wore smooth clothes and stood outside talking trash to Herbert and the weenagers, bragging on about all the places that he travelled.

"How you feelin', Mrs. Reeves?"

"I'm fine, Romello," she said, draping the fabric over him. "I'm telling you right now, I don't need none of your small talk today."

"Small talk! Mrs. Reeves, I'm more of a big talk kind of guy. Did I ever tell you about my trip down to Alabama—"

"No, and I don't want to hear it now—"

"I do," Portico interrupted. "I never been to Alabama. You took a plane?"

"Oh yeah!" Romello said, all puffed up.

"You were in the clouds?"

"*Above* the clouds."

"*Above* the clouds?" Portico couldn't believe it. If he wasn't already Stuntboy, he would've picked flying as his superpower. "And what's up there? Space?" he asked.

"Nope, more sky. Bluest you ever seen. Even if it's

raining down here, up there above them clouds, it's crystal clear. **But let me tell you about Alabama—"**

"There are birds up there? Like, above the clouds?"

"I don't know. I mean, who can pay attention to birds when you're in an airplane?"

"Wait, so tell me about the plane."

"Well, what you wanna know about the plane?"

"Did you fly it?"

Romello looked at Portico, wondering if maybe he was joking. But he wasn't. He really wanted to know if Romello was the pilot of the plane.

"Well . . . I mean . . . of course, I did," Romello said.

Mrs. Reeves slapped him on the back of the neck.
"Haircut's all done!" she said. Then she mumbled, "Liar."

Next up was Ms. Marcy, who loved to sing while getting her haircut. Then came Prince, a little little boy who pooped his pants, right in the chair. Gran Gran came to get her eyebrows trimmed, Brent Pollard came for a special design on the side of his head, and on and on, until finally, **the most interesting man walked up to the chair.**

SUPER

His name was Mr. Soup. When he stepped through the crowd, everyone called out for him.

"Soup!"

"Wassup, Soup!"

"Yo, Soup, I called you last week. **You too busy for me now?"**

"**Big Soup!** Hardest-working man in the building."

When he got to the chair, Soup—a giant in overalls and boots—sat down and took off his hat.

"What we doing today, Soup?" Mrs. Reeves asked.

"Whatever you want," he said.

As Portico's mum cut the hair of the man they called Soup, everyone came up to ask him things about the building. Things that only he knew. **It was like he was the**

real king of the castle. The wizard of Skylight
Gardens. Something like that. A person who knew where
the secret parts were and how it all worked. Everybody
respected him, except, apparently, for Herbert and the
weenagers, who cracked secret jokes about him. But they
crack jokes about everyone.

But the one thing that bothered Portico about Soup was
his name. Why Soup? I mean, maybe he just really
liked soup, which is definitely a good enough reason to name
yourself after something. Portico really liked Zola, and had
sometimes thought about calling himself Zola, but then he
figured she wouldn't like it because she didn't even like him
wanting to share the *Super Space Warriors* characters with
her. Point is, if it was soup that made Soup pick the name
Soup, Portico could understand. But he'd never seen Soup
eating soup. Never even heard him talk about it. So, while
Mrs. Reeves was snipping away his hair, Portico figured this
was the time to ask.

"Hey, Mr. Soup, can I ask you something?"

"Of course."

"Why we call you Soup? I mean, why is that your name?"

Soup smiled. "That's not my real name. My real name is Joe. Joe Munch. 'Soup' is short for 'super.'"

"SUPER?"

"Yeah, and 'super' is short for 'superintendent.'"

"Or, 'superintendent' is *long* for 'Super,'" Portico replied. This made more sense to him. "So, you're . . . a Super?"

"Yep. I'm a super."

"A *real* Super?"

Portico, bursting with head-blow-off excitement, waved his hand wildly to get Zola to stop on her 613th roller-skating lap from courtyard to lobby. She needed to hear this.

"He a Super!" Portico broke the news as Zola skated over fast fast.

"A . . . Super?" Zola was just as head-blow-off excited.

"Yep."

"But how?" Zola asked.

"Yeah, but how?" Portico followed.

From there, Soup told them all about working in different buildings and how he used to be a janitor at a middle school in a different city, a while ago.

"It was called Latimer Middle School," he said. "After that gig I became a Super."

"But what's it like to be a *real* Super?" Portico asked. Soup smiled again.

Portico couldn't believe
a Super, a **REAL Super,**
was living in his building.
He'd seen this man almost every
day, but had no clue! A *Super.*
He also couldn't understand
how so many other people knew.
Supers were supposed to stay
secret, weren't they? Had Portico
been getting it wrong this whole time?

> Being a super is just about taking care of things. Looking out for people. That's all.

Mrs. Reeves finished Soup's cut,
showed him the mirror, and sprayed a
cloud of the sneezy-sweet on his head.

"Let me ask you something,
Portico," Soup said. "You gon' follow in your mama's
footsteps and cut hair when you get older?"

Portico shrugged. He hadn't really thought about it, but now
he was thinking about it, and now that he was thinking about
it, it seemed pretty cool. **"Maybe,"** he said.

"Tell you what. You practice on your daddy's head a few
times, and then I'll let you cut mine. **I'll be your first**
paying customer." Soup shook Portico's hand.

"You a Super, so I'd cut your hair for free, *unless* your superpower is money, which if it is, I'll cut your hair for only a million dollars."

What Portico didn't know was that his first chance to practice would be a few hours later, after the line for haircuts had died down. Herbert hung around until the very end, then said he didn't want a cut. Zola was skated out and went home. And there were only a few people left. One of those people was Portico's father.

"Can I get a cut?" Mr. Reeves asked, as if he wasn't sure if Mrs. Reeves would do it.

"You know what, you can get one if you let Portico cut it."

"What?" Mr. Reeves squawked.

"Don't worry, I'll guide him."

Portico couldn't believe what he was hearing. He jumped up, ready to make it happen.

"**Wait, wait,**" said Mr. Reeves. "We gotta make some kind of deal first."

"**What kind of deal?**" asked Portico.

"If I let you cut my hair, you have to clean up all the hair on this floor," said Mr. Reeves. The thing is, there was hair everywhere. But Portico really wanted to cut his father's hair, because if he did, he was one step closer to cutting the Super's hair. "**Deal?**"

"**Deal.**"

HOW TO CUT YOUR FATHER'S HAIR

1. Terribly.
But everyone's gotta start somewhere.

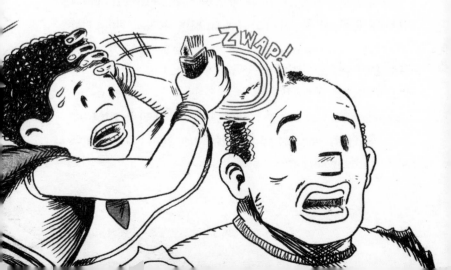

FROM HAIR TO THERE

After Portico swept up all the hair—*all* the hair—he headed back upstairs to see if maybe his father's haircut had calmed down some. I don't know if haircuts can calm down, but he was hoping so, because his dad's hair looked like it got some bad news. Which matched Portico's face, because you guessed it . . .

YOU GUESSED IT.

His parents were arguing. By the way, "arguing" is long for *"ARGH"*!

This time it wasn't over a table, or a picture frame, or a chair, or even a haircut (which would've made sense). This time it was over . . . a plate. Not a dinner plate or a tectonic plate (the weird things underground that cause earthquakes, though this was clearly causing an earthquake), but a plate that Portico made when he was in kindergarten. **An art project plate.**

See, when Portico was in kindergarten, he had this teacher, Mrs. Griffith, who had all the kids draw pictures on plates as gifts to their parents.

So, on his plate, he drew a family portrait. It looked like they were all smiling, but like it was one smile stretched across all their faces. **A uni-smile.**

On the bottom of the plate were the letters MLKJD, which stood for Martin Luther King Jr. Day, which is what this plate was a gift for. People usually don't give gifts for that holiday, but Mrs. Griffith thought it would be a great idea, and so did Portico. Mr. and Mrs. Reeves hung it on the wall, the only plate—besides Gran Gran's fancy plates from China—no one could ever eat on.

They loved it so much that now they were fighting over it.

"I'm his mother," Mrs. Reeves said.

"What does that mean—**only YOU** deserve the gifts he makes for *both* of us?"

agile

"**No**, I'm saying I'd love to have it."

"Well, I'd love to have it too. I mean, look at me. **I'm the biggest person in the picture.**"

"Because you're the biggest person in the house," Mrs. Reeves said. **"You also have the biggest mouth."**

"Oh yeah?"

"Yeah!"

Portico stood there, watching his parents throw insults back and forth, standing in front of the messy monster piles, which seemed to also be arguing with each other. Finally, Portico cleared his throat to get their attention.

"Oh, Portico. Didn't see you there."

"**You never do,**" he grumbled.

"I'm . . . sorry," his mother said.

"We both are."

"What y'all fighting about now?"

"It's nothing," his mother said, even though Portico was looking at the plate in both of their hands.

"**Um . . . listen,** we just need to sort this out. In the meantime maybe see if Zola is still skating," said his father.

"She's not."

"Well, go check again," his mother snapped.

WHERE'S THE SUPER WHEN YOU NEED HIM

When Portico got to Zola's, he was surprised she wasn't watching *Super Space Warriors*, like usual. Instead, she was knocking on the windows and tapping the walls and doing all kinds of weird stuff.

Ummm, Z? What you doin?

Checking for wrong stuff.

Wrong stuff?

"Yeah, like, checking to see if the walls are too thin. Or maybe if the glass in the windows is cracked." She kicked the radiator a few times. Then went to the bathroom just to flush the toilet over and over again.

"Zola, instead of flushing the toilet a hundred times, why don't you go test the kitchen sink. And while you're there, see if the water still washes dishes," Zola's father joked from the bedroom.

"But . . . why?" Portico asked.

"Because that's the only way we can get the Super to come visit."

This was a genius idea! The truth is, no one ever saw the Super. You had to call him, but first you had to have a reason to call him.

Wrong stuff.

"And what you gonna do when he gets here?"

"What you mean? I'm gonna ask him to teach me how to be a Super!" Zola turned the tap on. She squeezed in way too much soap and started scrubbing the dishes.

"I wonder if he has some kind of special powers to get my parents to stop fighting over the stuff in our house."

"Oh no, not again." Zola handed Portico a plate to dry. "Is that why you're here? The mean time?"

"Yeah."

"I thought it was because you were going to help me find a reason to call the Super," Zola said, handing Portico another plate.

"Well . . . that, too."

"What's the fight about this time?"

Portico didn't say. He just held the plate up.

"What . . . a plate?"

Portico explained about the plate. "I want to tell them to just give it to Gran Gran, but Gran Gran is Dad's mum, and so it'll be like giving it to Dad and my mum will be mad. But I can't say give it to A New Name Every Day, because technically that's my mum's cat, which means technically she'll have it. So I don't know what to do."

"Hmmm." Zola thought, handing Portico a glass.

"This is just like on **Episode 17** of

Super Space Warriors,

when Mater and Pater find out that their mother, before she died, left them a piece of the sun. She locked it in a special box and hid it underground. Have you seen that episode?"

"I don't think so," Portico said.

"It was a good one. Basically, she left them one of the most powerful things a sun protector could have. And Mater and Pater had decided to work together to find it, and they did. And when they finally opened it up, it was so beautiful that they both reached for it at the same time."

"Oh boy."

"The fight wasn't a long one because the piece of the sun slipped out of both of their hands. And do you know what would happen if a piece of the sun touched the Earth?"

Portico's beaner cleaners took the place of his think blob. Made his brain feel like it was shrinking. "You mean . . ."

Zola shook her head, squirted more soap. "I swear . . . I would be so much more careful if I were a sun protector, you know?" But before Zola could hand Portico the next dish, he was gone.

Portico torpedoed into his apartment. His parents were still going back and forth about the plate, and instead of trying to stop them, he did his famous Portico Punch. Well, it's not really that famous because he almost never does it. Actually, he's never done it. Ever. Not even one time before this moment. Which is why he had no idea his punch was a kick, and even less of a clue his leg would go up as high as it did—which was pretty impressive—but also that it would kick the plate out of his parents' hands.

It crashed onto the floor and shattered into a bunch of pieces. And as Stuntboy lost his balance, he crashed onto the floor too, landing right in front of the chunk of plate that had him on it. Smiling.

Episode 5

WHO ROCKS THE BLOCK

Roll the credits.
Cue the music.

I need everyone. EVERYONE. Big band. Let's make sure we have horns. Saxophones, trumpets, trombones, and flutes, even though I don't think flutes are horns. Bring them anyway. And drums. Lots of drums. The ones that go *boom de-boom boom*, and the ones that go *bang bang bang*, and the cymbals that sound like we're throwing rocks through windows. That's what we're gonna need for this episode. And do we have anyone who plays piano? Yeah? **Bring them in.** And a guitar, too. Oh, and get some kids from outside, and bring them in here to make fart noises or something. Hey, an instrument is an instrument.

Got it?
Good.
Let's sing the song.
And a one, and a two, and a...

DEFINITION OF A BLOCK PARTY

On the 189th day of Portico Reeves and Zola Brawner's best best friendship, the castle—well, not the castle itself but the grown-ups who live in the castle—threw a block party. Block parties happen every summer around here, but this was the first of the season.

DIFFERENCES BETWEEN A BLOCK PARTY AND A BIRTHDAY PARTY:

1. Oldies. They're everywhere at block parties. Playing cards, dancing weird like ancient children.

2. Instead of decorating with twenty balloons, decorate with big orange cones. Line them up at both ends of the block to keep cars from ruining the fun. (But keep balloons handy. You'll see why.)

3. Barbecue grills for food. I mean, you don't eat the grill, but you do eat the burnt hot dogs and sweaty hamburgers the grill makes.

4. Big rubbish bins. One for rubbish. One for drinks.

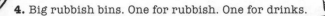

5. And the DJ has big outside speakers. The kind that drown out sirens and bus brakes. That pretty much makes block parties. A jam for the concrete kingdom.

The other thing about a block party is, two very important people have to show up on time. The first is . . .

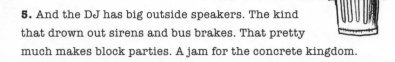

Mr. Chico has been living around here for as long as around here has been. Some people say he's **the skylight of Skylight Gardens.** He claims his grandfather built the castle, but don't nobody believe that. What we all believe is him saying he started DJ'ing a long long long time ago, back when hip-hop was just a baby, crawling around from neighbourhood to neighbourhood, city to city.

"It was all about the DJ. The rapper was second place to the person making the people move their feet. Don't nobody care what you got to say if it don't make them move," he'd say. Mr. Chico would tell stories about spinning and scratching records, turning songs into sound effects, but none of it really mattered to the kids of this castle. What they cared about was the music. **Just the music.** Mr. Chico did all the parties for anyone who lived here, including Zola's birthday party, but we won't talk about that because . . . **I'm sure you remember what happened.**

So, like always, Mr. Chico was supposed to DJ the block party. He'd set up his equipment early in the morning—turntables, speakers, microphone—but now he was nowhere to be found. Portico asked Mr. Tony, who owns the snack truck parked outside the building, if maybe he'd seen him.

"Nah, I ain't seen him. He's probably stumbling around here somewhere."

But where? All the castlemates were outside, everyone ready to get the party started, but you can't have a party without music.

An hour passed and still no Mr. Chico, which meant an hour of a **musicless not-party,** an hour of Syl and Byl begging people to play dodgeball, which meant an hour of Portico hitting **the Zamarama Zigzag in the ziggiest and zaggiest of ways,** pretty much saving everyone from getting their faces stinged and zinged by dodgeballs. **And because the job of Stuntboy is**

never done, Portico decided Stuntboy might have to DJ, too. I mean, that's the only way to save Mr. Chico (why was he always saving Mr. Chico?). But as Portico made his way through the crowd, a voice came through the speakers. **A familiar voice.**

"**Um . . . check check.** Good afternoon, y'all. I don't know where Chico at, but that's okay. **I happen to know a little something about DJ'ing.**"

"**Yo, is that . . .**" Zola's mouth dropped open.

"**Gran Gran?**" Portico's mouth dropped open too.

Yep, it was his grandma standing behind the turntables.

"**Gran Gran, what you doing?**" asked Portico, now behind the DJ table.

"*DJ* **Gran Gran, to you.** And I'm here to rock the party, which I can do because my eyes are finally fully rested." Gran Gran had been resting her eyes for, I don't know, six years.

"But do you know what you doing?" Portico asked. And instead of answering, Gran Gran started to scratch the records and jam. She did all kinds of tricks, and the block finally became **a party**.

The line dancing started.
　The burnt hot dogs were passed out.
　　The soggy burgers too.
　　　Ketchup and mustard.
　　　　Juice boxes from the bin.
　　　　　Juice boxes into the (other) bin.

THE SPECIAL WRENCH

The other important person who has to show up to the block party on time is Portico's father. Not because he was a bin man and there was guaranteed to be a lot of rubbish at the party. But because he somehow had a special wrench. THE special wrench. It was one of the many things Portico loved about him. The first, of course, was that he was a bin man, and there was nothing cooler than a rubbish truck, except the man who hangs off the side, cleaning up the neighbourhood. Second was the fact that his father also didn't like peas and carrots. And third, his father had the special wrench. No one was sure if it came with working on a rubbish truck, some kind of fancy tool in case you have to fix that monster mouth in the back of the truck, or what. All everyone knew was that wrench happened to be the perfect size for opening the fire hydrant. And that's what he did.

Mr. Reeves went to the hydrant on the block, attached that wrench to it, and yanked it loose. And as soon as the cap came off, out poured the water.

Which meant now the block party, was a water party.

SPLASH

Not just any water party, but a water **balloon** party.

(See? Gotta keep balloons handy!) And water balloon parties are the best.

As all the kids ran around soaking one another with water, or drinking out of the tap like Stump (who in the world is . . . nevermind), the weenagers, especially Herbert Singletary the Worst, filled balloon after balloon like they were planning some kind of attack. And they were. **As soon as they had enough—had to be at least thirty balloons!—they . . . ATTACKED!**

Balloons in the air! Balloons in the air! Splashing down on the heads of everyone.

Kids scattered all over the block, trying to escape the wet. But once Herbert Singletary the Worst saw Portico and Zola, he locked in and went after them, specifically. They ran toward the end of the block. When they got to the cones—the orange barrier—they turned around to try to reason with Herbert.

THERE'S NO WAY TO REASON WITH HERBERT

"Come on, man," Portico said, hands up. "Let us go."
But Herbert had that look on his face. He had that jokey-jaw, teasy-teeth, haha-head mean look on his face. Oh, and his eyebrows were meaner than ever.

"Why would I do that?" he said.

Zola stepped up. "Know what? Do what you gotta do." Then she turned to Portico, who was preparing to jump in front of her, and stopped him. **"It's just water."** And as soon as she turned back, her face met the balloon. Well, really the balloon met her face, like, *Hello my name is* . . . *SPLASH!*

Actually, it was more like . . .

KA-SPLOOOOOSHHHHHHHHH!!!

So, it *was* just water. But not water like in a shower. Or like a bath. Or like the rain. It was sting-y water. Water that felt like fire when it hit Zola's face. Her glasses flew off and hit the ground. *CRACK!* Zola held her cheek, and Portico—whose insides were piling, jumbling, mixing, whose think blob and beat box were fighting—picked up Zola's glasses. Handed them to her. Then looked at Herbert Singletary the Worst.

"You next," Herbert said.

Usually, Portico would've run. But he knew he'd failed on his stunt work.

He was supposed to jump in and take the hit. He *tried*, but Zola stopped him. He should've tried harder. But he didn't. And now the stunts were over for the day.

Portico glared at Herbert in a way he'd never glared at anyone.

"You *mad*?" Herbert taunted. "What you gon' do about it?" Herbert cocked his arm back, aiming the next balloon at Portico's face. And Portico charged.

IF ONLY TELEPORTATION WAS REAL

Once Portico was pulled off Herbert Singletary by his parents, they hauled him back upstairs. It all happened so fast. The tackle. The snatch-up. The escort into the building. It was like a blur. Like he had teleported.

"Sit down," Mr. Reeves said.

Portico sat on the floor.

"On the sofa, son," Mrs. Reeves said. And after Portico sat on the sofa, she asked him what happened and why he jumped on Herbert.

"He threw a balloon at Zola's face and broke her glasses."

"Then you did what?" asked Portico's mum.

Portico didn't answer.

"We know what you did. We *saw* it," she said.

"But I was sticking up for her."

"**How?** What if he had left her and she kept getting hit with balloons?" asked Portico's dad.

"He should've taken her with him. Or called out for one of us," said Portico's mum.

"But in the moment he wasn't thinking about that. He did what he should've done," said his dad.

"I don't want my son to think fighting is the answer," said his mum.

"It wasn't fighting; it was defense," said his dad.

"It wasn't defense because he wasn't even being attacked," said his mum.

"But his best friend was attacked." Dad.

"And now you're attacking me." Mum.

"No, *you're* attacking *me*." Dad.

And the back and forth kept going.

Before Portico could even find out if he would be grounded or not, his parents were in a full-on argument.

"I just don't want our son to be mean!"

"He wasn't being mean!"

But now they were being mean to each other. So mean they didn't even notice the knocking on the door. So mean they didn't even notice the door open. So mean they didn't even notice Gran Gran coming in with Zola. So mean they didn't even notice Zola walking down the hall to Portico's room, where Portico was now sitting on the floor with A New Name Every Day, fidgeting with a magnifying glass and a roll of plastic wrap.

"Hey," Zola said, holding her broken glasses.

"Hey."

"Hey," she repeated. "Um . . . so . . . Herb—"

"Don't say his name."

"O . . . kay." Zola sat down on the floor. "But I was just gonna say that if that was a stunt, maybe you could call it the Herbert-Hitter-Block-Party-Balloon-Buster Crusher."

"Please, Zola." Portico wasn't amused. "Don't say his name."

"Well, can I say your parents' names, because they seem to—"

"Nope."

"But they got those big piles of stuff out there that look like they're gonna—"

"Nope." Portico shook his head. He didn't want to talk about the piles because they scared him. They'd been getting bigger by the day. Every time his parents fought over a new thing, the piles grew.

"Mean time," Zola said. "Got it."

"Yep."

Zola sighed. "Well, at least tell me what you doing?"

Portico looked up. "At first, I was working on building a teleportation machine," he explained.

"To go where?"

"I don't know. Maybe Alabama." Portico shrugged. "But now I'm working on a way to fix your glasses glass."

"What?"

Portico jumped up, repeated himself. "I'm working on a way to fix your glasses glass. I don't know how to put see-better stuff in it, but this will at least make things look big." He reached for her glasses and went to work.

"Don't worry about it," Zola said. "My mum's gonna take me to get 'em fixed tomorrow."

But Portico insisted, and a few minutes later, he was done. "Try that." Zola put them on. "Better?"

"Ummm . . ."

"I knew it would work!"

"Well . . ." Zola looked like she was trying to find the right words to describe what she was seeing. "Here, you try 'em."

Portico put them on.

"How you feel?" asked Zola.

"Like the world is . . . mixed-up," he said. "Like I'm looking inside my own head."

"Yeah, and your living room is quiet, which is just as weird."

When Portico and Zola went to see what all the hush was about, Portico's parents were sitting on the sofa, the two towers of stuff casting shadows on the room. Silent. But not angry silent.

Sad silent.

The good news is, WE (not me, but someone!) FOUND MR. CHICO! He'd come into their apartment and was sitting at the kitchen table.

"Hey, babies," said Gran Gran.

"What's going on?" asked Portico.

"Just getting Mr. Chico here to pay me for my DJ'ing gig."

"But what about . . . *them*?" Portico pointed to his parents.

"Oh, don't you worry about them. They on punishment. Grounded!"

COMMERCIAL BREAK: This commercial is brought to you by

HOW TO GROUND PARENTS

Please don't try. You can't.

Sorry. But . . . call your grandparents.

Now back to your regularly scheduled program.

ONE MAN'S RUBBISH CHUTE IS ANOTHER MAN'S TIME MACHINE

Roll credits.
Cue music.

All bells, please. I need *ring-a-ling-a-lings* only. Just the triangle and the xylophone. Oof. Another one of those Xs. I have no idea what to do when the X is at the beginning of the word. How do you say it?

Is it ex-ile-a-phone? I don't think it is. But . . . do we have one? Can we please get one in here for the theme song? We need an ex-ile-a-phone to really take this thing up a notch!

And don't forget the triangle. I'm serious. It won't work without the triangle.

Let's hit it!

And a one, and a two,
and a . . .

SATURDAY MORNING FEVER

This is Portico Reeves. This is his mother, Sasha Reeves, or as we know her, Mrs. Reeves or Portico's mum. Usually, Portico would be practicing his stunt moves for his other (secret, not so secret anymore) identity as Stuntboy. But on Saturdays, the only stunt he's allowed to do is . . . **chores.**

Chores stink. Why did he have to wake up early, separate his white clothes from his dark clothes (which he always thought was a little weird), then clean the bathroom with some stuff that made him feel like someone poured pepper in his nose? Then he had to dust all the tables and chairs in the apartment, which also made him feel like someone poured pepper in his nose. He didn't even really understand what dust was. **Where did it come from?** Also, why do you have to dust . . . the dust? Then Portico had to vac- uum, and maybe that was because he'd just knocked all the dust onto the floor. That, and all the cat hair. Luckily, he actually kind of liked vacuuming. I mean, **the vacuum cleaner was a big, truck-faced machine** that was loud enough to drown out his mother's oldie music that she played every Saturday morning.

She called it cleaning music.

He called it *Do We Really Have to Listen to This* music.

Portico pushed the vacuum around the house, bumping into his parents' argument piles, trying not to knock them over because that would cause a new argument. He imagined all the things being sucked into the cleaner, like tiny speck people who lived in the dust-land on the floor, being inhaled into this roaring spaceship.

VRRRRMMM VRRRRMMMM

On this particular Saturday, halfway through the job, he heard his mother screaming his name. He could barely hear her over the vacuum. *And* the music.

"You ain't hear me calling you?" she said. Portico shook his head. "Zola's here." And before Portico could even say anything, his mother continued, "But don't think you get to quit your chores. Matter fact, Zola, you can help."

"But I'm basically done," Portico replied.

"Hmmmm." His mother scratched her chin. "Let me inspect."

Oh no. Inspecting was the worst part of the Saturday morning—**worst than the music and all the scrubbing**—because it was basically Portico's mum looking for all the things he didn't clean well enough. She checked the bathtub, the toilet, the sink. She ran her fingers across all the furniture to make sure there was no dust left behind. She even checked the floor to make sure Portico had vacuumed right. And there was one place where Portico always always always forgot: the corners.

"Look at this," she said, kneeling. **"Dust bunnies. So you're definitely *not* done."**

171.

CARE FOR
HOW TO CLEAN UP DUST BUNNIES

Usually, Portico would just sweep in all the corners and be done with it. But Zola was there. Standing right next to him. So . . . **things changed.**

"Why you think they call 'em dust bunnies?" Portico asked.

Zola shrugged. "I mean, they don't really look like bunnies."

"And they not cuddly like bunnies, either."

"Definitely not," Zola said, leaning in closer. **"Maybe it's because"**—she took a deep breath—**"they HOP!"** She blew on the ball of dust, and it bounced across the floor. Well, it sort of bounced. Let's just say it bounced. Portico blew it next, and

it bounced farther. And before they knew it, they had gathered other dust bunnies from other parts of the house and made a whole *fluffle* of dust bunnies.

They named them all. Snowball, Hair Clump, Weirdo, Rugs Bunny, and even got a few baby carrots from the fridge to feed the new pets. I mean, someone's gotta eat 'em, right? But that was the biggest mistake, because when Mrs. Reeves came back to inspect again, instead of seeing clean, she saw a pile of dust *and* food on the floor.

"Portico Reeves and Zola Brawner! Have y'all lost y'all minds? Have the aliens from that show y'all watch come into my home and crawled into your heads?"

COMMERCIAL BREAK: This commercial is brought to you by

QUESTIONS MOMS ASK THAT YOU'RE NOT SUPPOSED TO REALLY ANSWER

1. Those

Now back to your regularly scheduled program.

So, broom, meet dustpan. Dust bunnies, meet rubbish.

"Now, take that rubbish out, and then you're all done with your chores," Mrs. Reeves said.

"Finally," Portico said under his breath.

"What you say?" *(See previous commercial break.)*

"Nothin'."

TALKING RUBBISH

Rubbish chutes are cool. I mean, minus the rubbish part. But, come on, there's something so interesting about a slot you put rubbish in, and then the rubbish goes somewhere, but no one knows where. Portico always hoped it was a portal or a time machine that took it all to another dimension. I mean, how else could all these people make all this rubbish, and the whole planet—at least his apartment building—ain't completely drowning in it.

In Skylight Gardens, on the fourth floor, the rubbish chute is at the end of the hallway. Portico and Zola dragged the bags of rubbish down the hall, opened the chute, and tossed the bags in.

TRASH CHUTE

"Look out below!"

Portico did that every time he tossed the rubbish—something his father used to do—and waited for someone to answer. **But no one ever did.**

Then, to his surprise, a voice said, **"Why don't you jump in next."**

Portico stuck his head in the chute. **"Is someone down there?"**

"*You* should be," the voice said. This time, Portico and Zola realized it was coming from a *different* kind of rubbish chute, one attached to a weenager: **Herbert Singletary the Worst.**

"Oh *no*," Zola groaned, now realizing he was coming toward them.

"Come on, Herbert. It's Saturday, don't you wanna take the day off?" asked Portico.

"Okay, let's make a deal," said Herbert. "If y'all jump down that rubbish chute, I'll leave both of you alone. Forever."

Portico and Zola looked at each other.

"Umm . . . I don't know, man." Zola was unsure. But Portico had already opened the chute and was trying to figure out how he could fit his body in it. He always kinda wanted to jump down the rubbish chute anyway. Plus, he felt like his father would be down there to catch him. Or maybe the chute would send him back to the past, back to when the things in his apartment were just treated like things, and the people in his apartment were treated like family. This would surely be his greatest stunt ever. But as he stuck his head in, another voice came barreling down the hallway. A big voice.

Li'l Herby!

Portico pulled his head
out of the chute, only to find . . .
no . . . couldn't be . . .
THE SUPER!

Had he come to save Portico and Zola on the 195th day of
their best best friendship? But who called him? How did he
know they needed his help?

Herbert rolled his eyes, huffed.

"I've been looking for you," said the Super.

"Well, you found me."

"It's Saturday, and you know your mother
wants you to do your chores." The Super put his

hand on Herbert's shoulder, but Herbert pulled away. Portico just couldn't believe Herbert had to do chores on Saturday too. "I'll give you ten minutes to finish up with your friends, then get yourself back downstairs and help straighten up the place. If you won't do it for me, do it for your mum."

Wait . . . was the Super one of Herbert's . . . parents? Couldn't be, could it? But . . . who-what-when-where-why . . . *howwwwww?*

Portico dropped his jaw, and it felt like he'd dropped his brain.

Herbert dropped his head. Nodded. And the Super was gone.

WHO IS HERBERT SINGLETARY THE WORST (REALLY?)

Herbert walked back down the hall toward the half door.

"Wait. Herbert, wait!" Portico called out. He and Zola were so confused.

Finally, Herbert stopped. "What?"

"So . . . the Super . . . he . . . um . . . your . . . um . . ." Portico couldn't find the words to ask how Herbert Singletary the Worst could be related to a SUPER.

"He's the only reason I live in this dump," Herbert spat.

"What you mean?"

"I mean, he married my mum and moved us in here. Away from my house. My room. My neighbourhood. My friends. To be around . . . you."

"Where's your dad?" Portico asked, even though having a super-dad seemed like a fair trade.

"Who knows. Maybe your father picked him up and threw him in the trash, like I almost did you."

Normally, Portico would be mad at the insult, but at the moment he couldn't even hear it. His mind was too busy erupting. "At least your new dad is a Super. That means you can probably be a Super, too!"

Herbert didn't respond; he just kept walking to the half door.

that mean the Super lives there too? And, and if the Super lives there, why he tell you to do chores *downstairs?*"

Herbert opened **the half door wide**, revealing a room that looked like the inside of a robot. Tubes and tanks and bigger tubes (pipes).

"It's a boiler room," Herbert said. "My real apartment is downstairs. With him."

Happy? No. But to Portico, a boiler room seemed fitting for a guy like Herbert. I mean, where else could he go boil?

"Oh, that's cool. I love boiler rooms," Portico said quickly. Not that he'd ever been in a boiler room.

"Can we come in?" Zola asked.

"NO!"

The next thing that had to happen was both Portico and Zola had to tell their parents what they'd just found out. That the Super is Herbert Singletary the Worst's new father. **Weird. Like**
     of ALL the people who got to have super-parents,
     of ALL the people who might grow up to be super
     because of a super-parent,
     of ALL the people who might grow a real deal superpower . . .

HERBERT *STINKIN'* SINGLETARY
THE *STINKIN'* WORST?

It was unfair, but still pretty cool.

Zola walked one door to the right. Portico walked one door to the left. But when Portico went into his apartment to tell his parents the news, they were having a very intense conversation about a clock. Okay, it wasn't an intense conversation. **You know what it was.**

"You don't even like clocks!" Mrs. Reeves said. "If I hadn't taken it off the wall to dust it, you never would've noticed it."

"I love clocks! Love 'em! I love clocks so much that I'm constantly thinking about when our time is UP!"

"Oh, I love clocks *more*. You know what I keep thinking about? How much time I've wasted!"

"I'm so tired of this."

"*I'm* so tired of this."

Then more from Portico's mum. And more from his dad. And more from his mum. And more from his dad. And Gran Gran woke up for a moment, checked her watch, then went back to resting her eyes. Even she was tired of this.

Finally, Portico, who'd been waiting for them to finish so he could tell them all about how Herbert Singletary the Worst might actually one day become Herbert Singletary the Super because his new father is a Super, spoke up. Maybe a better way to put it is, he screamed:

"I think you both need a time-out!"

His parents turned to him. At first, Portico thought his mother would ask him another one of those questions about whether or not he had misplaced his mind. But she didn't.

"Sorry, Port," she said. "You're right."

"We just need to, I don't know, figure out what to do with this clock," his father explained.

"Listen," his mother chimed. "Why don't you—"

"I know, I know. Go see Zola."

Zola was in the middle of telling the Herbert story to her mother. Well, she started with the half door next door.

"It's called a boiler room. Did you know that?" Zola asked as Portico took a seat on the edge of Zola's chair. "Herbert hides in there."

"We're all hiding from something," Mrs. Brawner said. She always says stuff like that.

Zola went on telling her mother about how Portico almost jumped down the rubbish chute until the Super saved him and gave up the secret of all secrets (well . . . *ahem* . . . the second biggest secret because the whole Stuntboy thing is the first biggest) that Mr. Soup, the Super, was Herbert's. New. Dad.

"I wish I had a Super for my dad. Or a boiler room," Portico said.

"What's wrong, Portico?" Mrs. Brawner asked.

"Nothing."

"Whenever he gets like this, it's because his parents are in the mean time," Zola explained.

Mrs. Brawner nodded. "Should we meditate?"

"I don't really feel like breathing through my toes right now."

"How about some yoga?"

"What flavour?"

Zola laughed. "Not yogurt. *Yoga*. It's like special stretching."

"It'll make you feel better," Zola's mum said.

They moved the lawn chairs to make space in the living room.

"Let's start with the first pose. It's called downward-facing dog." Silly name. Upward-facing cat would've been better. But whatever.

From there they went from pose to pose, stretch to stretch, breathing in and breathing out. It was like meditation'ing while moving.

There was **warrior pose, and cobra pose, and goddess pose,** and Portico's favorite, **hero pose**.

"Breathe," Mrs. Brawner whispered. "Feel your breath, feel your heart beating in your chest like a clock, the clock of your life."

And that did it. Brought Portico right back to what had caused the mean time, this time.

"Zola," Portico whispered.

"Breathe," Zola said.

I AM BREATHING, BUT I'M ALSO WORRIED ABOUT MY PARENTS. THEY'RE FIGHTING OVER AN OLD CLOCK.

AN OLD CLOCK?

"Kinda like SUPERSPACE WARRIORS Episode 42?"

"What happened on Episode 42?!"

"Shhhhh," Zola's mum said. "Focus."

Portico and Zola *were* focused, just on a different thing:
Episode 42.

"Okay, so remember that weird episode—"

"Every episode is weird."

"**I know.** But not weird like Episode 42, because that's when Mater and Pater make it to the planet of the Irators. And when they get there, they get captured and put in this jail thing. But it wasn't really like a jail. It was just a room.

And they called it

TIME."

"Oh, yeah! That empty room with the door at the end of the hallway that kept moving closer and closer to them."

"Right. Well, it *was* moving closer and closer, at first. But then when they tried to run out of it, they could never get to it. They would run toward the door, but the door would get farther and farther away with every step."

"And they were trapped."

"**But they weren't.** As soon as they stopped running toward the door, the door started coming closer and closer and closer and closer again, until the whole room basically disappeared around them, and they were free."

"But because they were so worried about running out of TIME, **by the time they were free,** they were too tired to move."

"And the Irators were long gone, closing in on the sun, which was now left unprotected. All the **Super Space Warriors** had had to do was sit still.

But now they had to face the potential of an

EXPLOSION OF GREAT MAGNITUDE!"

"Shhhh," Mrs. Brawner hissed again.

"And now my parents are unprotected," Portico said. He couldn't focus on his breathing anymore because his squigglies seemed to be clogging up his taste tunnel. The frets were on full inside-mixup!

"Well, not exactly," said Zola.

"And . . . they both kept saying how tired they are," Portico explained. The frets fretting more.

"But maybe they mean tired in a different way. You know how people say they tired, but they really mean hungry," Zola tried to explain. "They're probably just hungry."

But fully fretted Portico was already out the door. Stuntboy had left the building.

Okay, not the building, but Apartment 4E.

ABOUT TIME

Stuntboy came back into his apartment, and his parents

were prepared for him to do his usual rolls and tumbles and flips and kicks, but instead, this time, in the mean time, he was in time, and on time, so he calmly walked into the middle of the living room and performed his **newest stunt**:

A hero pose.

He got down, closed his eyes, took a deep breath. In and blew it out. In, and blew it out. And the apartment became so silent, they could hear that the clock wasn't even ticking. **Wasn't working at all.**

Episode 7

SPOILER ALERT: For this episode, we'll hold the credits and music until the end.

THERE'S A MOVIE?

On the 200th day of Portico Reeves and Zola Brawner's best best friendship, the most amazing thing happened.

came out in theaters, and the dads, Mr. Reeves and Mr. Brawner, took Portico and Zola to see it.

First things first. Portico did at least thirty stunts on the way. A lot of Floppity-Flips over fire hydrants. Lots of Zamaramas and Jumbo Jumps when crossing streets. It was like he was playing out what he imagined the movie would be on the way to seeing what the movie would be. And Zola narrated the whole thing, which sounded like:

And then Portico ducked! Look out for that rocket!

Which was cut off by Mr. Reeves—let's call him Narrator #2—saying, "Portico, there's a car coming. Please stop playing around before I make you hold my hand."

And superheroes don't hold hands.

Second things second. SNACKS:

There were four people, which means they had to get two medium popcorns.

One for Zola and Portico.
One for the dads.

(Alternative: nachos, but WARNING, they'll be gone before the movie even starts!)

Candy. Some people put it in the popcorn. But not Portico and Zola. They both like to go back and forth—a little popcorn, a little candy, a little popcorn, a little candy, so that they'd leave the theater with some leftover of each stuck between their teeth. For the walk home.

Four drinks. There's something about movie theater soda that's more burpy than regular soda, which makes it twice as good because you get to taste it on the way down and on the way up.

SNACKS *NOT* TO GET:

Hot dogs. Just don't eat movie theater hot dogs. **Ever.**
(Shhhhh! The movie is starting.)

In the year 2099, Mater and Pater, the

Super Space Warriors, are in their lab, working on ways to defeat the Irators. But they still haven't learned to get along, and the Irators have taken advantage of their sibling rivalry.

If the Irators can't stand the heat, which is why they're trying to put out the sun, why don't we just go to their planet and use our Super Space Flamethrowers to kill them?

That's a ridiculous idea. We can't use fire in space, because there's no oxygen up there.

It would work. The fires just wouldn't be flames. They'd be fireballs. And, they'd be almost invisible. Which for us, is a good thing. Not so ridiculous now, huh?

Because they'd never see them coming?

(86 minutes later)

Roll the credits:

    Produced by Jason Reynolds

    Written by Jason Reynolds

        Directed by
    Raúl the Third and Elaine Bay

Soundtrack by fart noises and burps

A special thanks to all who watched,
    which is everyone EXCEPT for
    Portico Reeves and Zola Brawner,
who fell asleep after the first five
minutes of this movie because they
        were so excited to see it,
        they stayed awake all night.

LET THE BEGGING AND BUGGING BEGIN

"Can you *please, pleeeease, pleeeeeeease* tell us what happened?" Portico asked his father as they left the theater.

"Well, there was some space, and some warriors, and . . . an

AN EXPLOSION OF GREAT MAGNITUDE!

The rest you had to see to understand." Mr. Reeves laughed. He thought it was so funny that Portico and Zola slept through it all. Mr. Brawner laughed too.

"I just don't understand why y'all didn't wake us up," Zola said.

And both Mr. Reeves and Mr. Brawner said at the same time, **"WE TRIED!"**

But not hard enough. And now Portico and Zola were left wondering what happened in the movie. When they got back to the castle, they sat outside on the bench and talked about all the possibilities.

"Okay, so here's what I'm thinking," Portico said. "Maybe in the middle of all the fighting between the Super Space Warriors about how they're going to attack the Irators on their own planet with fire, the Irators attack the sun, and they have to change their plans."

"But they can't decide on what the new plan is," Zola said.

"Because they can never decide on anything."

"Right, so they go see their mother."

"On the show their mum ain't alive."

"I know," Zola said. "But maybe *that's* the twist. In the movie, maybe we find out she *is*, and she can put them in therapy to get them back on track so they can protect the sun."

"But then, maybe the mum is like, 'Y'all still haven't learned, so let me do it myself.' And she goes and kicks the butts of all the Irators and chases them back to their planet," said Portico.

"Then she takes Mater and Pater up in the *Sunjet*, and they go light the sun again," said Zola.

"The end."

That was the first idea. But there were more, especially from Zola. And after a whole bunch of brainstorming, Herbert Singletary the Worst showed up. Oh no!

"What y'all talking about?" Herbert asked.

"Oh, just how we need to go inside," Portico said, immediately feeling the frets.

"Come on," Herbert said. "I'm being serious." He was serious? He was always serious. Serious about being a bummer-beast. Hard to know if he was even being serious. About being serious. About wanting to know what Portico and Zola were talking about.

Zola sighed. "Just the new *Super Space Warriors* movie. We went today, but fell asleep right at the beginning and missed the whole thing."

Herbert started laughing.

HA! And laughing.

HA! And laughing.

HA! And . . . **you get the point.**

"You mean to tell me y'all missed the part at the end when they [redacted]."

"Whatever," Portico said. "You haven't seen it."

"Yes I have."

"Haven't."

"Have. **Forreal.** Been
my favourite show
since before
it was even
popular."

Portico was so mad that he ran from the bench, into the building, and didn't even wait for the elevator to go up. He just ran up the steps to the fourth floor and into his apartment, because if there was anyone he needed to talk to about this, it was his dad. He just wanted to make sure Herbert wasn't tricking him. I mean, he was the Worst, after all.

THE TURNUP

But when Portico charged through the front door, his parents were standing on opposite ends of the TV.

"Listen, you know I paid for this TV," his mother said.

"But I picked it out. You don't even watch TV," his father replied.

"So, because you picked it out, that means you get to have it?"

"You know I can't sleep without the TV on."

"That's not my fault!"

"Or maybe it is!"

208

They each had a hand on the television, and it looked like they'd pick it up any minute, and if that happened, there wasn't a stunt in the world that could save it, because it was definitely going to be dropped, and definitely going to be broken. And a broke TV equals a lot of boring days. Days chasing dust bunnies, or worse, reading!

So, instead of doing what he always did—what they always told him to do, which was go find Zola—Portico did something different. He grabbed the remote and turned the TV on.

"All I'm saying is, I spent my money on this. It belongs to me," his mother said.

Portico turned the channel. Thankfully, *Super Space Warriors* was about to come on after this commercial.

COMMERCIAL BREAK: This commercial is brought to you by

HOW TO MUTE YOUR PARENTS

First thing you have to do is turn the TV up.
A little louder. A liiiiiiittle louder.
There you go. You've done it!

Oh, and if you've got a cool grandma, you can take turns doing it.
Trust me, she wants to mute them too.
Might even give you strawberry sweets and everything.

Now back to your regularly scheduled program.

Oh, and for Stuntboy, this *definitely* counts as a stunt.

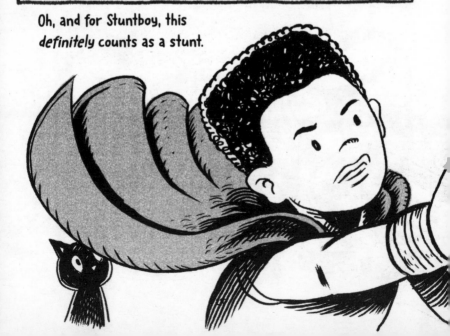

SUPER SPACE WARRIORS THEME MUSIC, IN THE KEY OF MAD

They're Suuuuuuper Space Warriors
They're Suuuuuuper Space Warriors
They don't get along, but don't get me wrong,
They're Suuuuuuper Space Warriors.

"Oh it's your money now?

I thought it was *our* money!"

Irators on the run, till the mission is done.
And even though it's no fun,
they have to protect the sun.
They're Suuuuuuper Space
Warriors.

KLICK
KLICK
KLICK

"It was. But now it's not. And because it's not, this TV is mine!"

THEY HAVE TO PROTECT THE SUNNNNNN!

EPISODE 8

SWEATING THE SMALL STUFF

Roll the credits.
Cue the music.

No, wait. WAIT! No instruments for this one. Let's just get an oldie to whistle, like they do on old TV shows. Something kinda sweet.

Now the song.

And a one,
and a two,
and a...

WeLLLLLLcoMe to
StUNtboyYYyy in the
MeaNNnnNnTIme!

KNOCK KNOCK

There's a time in every hero's life where they have to face the villain. **No running. No chasing. Just a face-to-face battle.** Okay, in Stuntboy's case, maybe it didn't need to be a *battle*. **But at least a clash.** Okay, maybe not a clash, but at least a . . .

Okay, fine. Stuntboy knocked on the half door.

But not before he got Zola. Can't venture into these kinds of territories alone. That would be silly. I know what you're thinking. You're thinking, why in the world, on the **204th** day of their best best friendship, would Portico and Zola knock on the half door?

Why would they bother the troll of all trolls, Herbert Singletary the Worst?

LOST AND FOUND, UNFORTUNATELY

It all started when Portico found an earring in the hall. He wasn't looking for it, that's for sure, but he was on his way to the postbox downstairs, which meant he was practicing the Untied Glide in the hallway, and saw it shining on the floor. He figured the person who lost it would come back for it, so he left it. But it was still there when he got back, a speck of glitter he couldn't ignore. So, he started knocking on doors to see whose earring it might've been.

Was it Mama Gloria's?

"Let me see it," she said. Mama Gloria examined it, then told Portico how she bet it was Ms. Majesty Morris's up on the top floor. "She think she so fancy because she live up there. I hear it's nice."

"It is," Portico said.

"Uh-huh," Mama Gloria said. "Well, how 'bout I hold on to this and take it on up there to her."

But Portico wouldn't let go of the earring—he knew how Mama Gloria was—and instead, moved on to the next door.

Was it Syl's or Byl's?

"Boy, you know how dangerous it is to wear earrings and have a rubber ball zooming toward your face like an asteroid?" said Syl.

"Better yet, you know how dangerous it is to wear earrings and throw a ball at someone's face as hard as you possibly can?" said Byl.

"Um . . . I . . . no. No, I don't."

And it wasn't Mr. Richmont's. Or Mrs. Richmont's.

Peanut Butter Jones wasn't home.

And it wasn't Zola's. Or Gran Gran's.

Or Mrs. Brawner's. Or Mr. Brawner's.

And it wasn't Portico's mother's.

And Portico's father didn't wear earrings.

Which left one person,
            and one person only.

A STRANGE INVITATION

Like I said, Portico and Zola knocked on the half door. No one answered, so they knocked again. Still nothing. Then they knocked one more time. And the door clicked and opened just slightly. An eye peered through the crack.

"Ugh," Herbert said. **"What y'all want?"**

"This yours?" Portico held the earring up like a precious jewel.

Herbert opened the half door—the boiler room door—more. **"Yeah, that's mine. What you doing with it?"**

"Found it on the floor out here."

No one will ever know what made Herbert do the strangest, most random, unexpected, too-weird-for-TV thing anyone on the fourth floor (well, really just Portico and Zola) had ever seen, but he said, **"Y'all . . . want to come in?"** Guess that was his way of saying thank you.

"No," said Zola.

"Yes," said Portico. He wasn't sure why. Maybe he just really wanted to see a boiler room.

Maybe because he knew Herbert liked *Super Space Warriors*. **Either way, he said yes, and he meant it.**

THE BOILER ROOM

The inside of a boiler room looks like the inside of a robot brain. **And it's hot.**

"Is it always this hot in here?" Zola asked.

"It's called a boiler room, so . . . yeah. But you get used to it," Herbert said. **"Gotta get tough enough to handle it, like me."** Herbert put his earring back in. "It's like when I first got this earring. You know I did it myself, right? Just punched a hole right through my own ear. **Didn't even cry."**

COMMERCIAL BREAK: This commercial is brought to you by

WHAT REALLY HAPPENED WHEN HERBERT SINGLETARY GOT HIS EAR PIERCED

He cried. I mean, he CRIED.

His mother said he sounded like a screaming cat. But, take it from me, he did not.

Now back to your regularly scheduled program.

"What about these pipes. What they do?" Portico asked, looking around the room.

"What you mean? They're perfect for working out." Herbert jumped up and grabbed one, started doing pull-ups.

This was good because the castle had everything except a gym. Most people worked out outside, but Herbert figured out how to exercise inside. He went on and on about the perks of the boiler room. The rumbling sound was like a purring cat, cozy, like the building snoring. I don't believe that, but that's what he said. He also said the steam was like one of those fancy rich people places that blow steam all over your body, and it makes you feel brand-new. Portico didn't understand that, but Herbert swore this was a real thing.

"I've got everything I need here," Herbert said. "Except all that noise coming from next door."

"That's probably my folks," Zola explained. "My dad's always practicing his lawn chair sales pitch, which by the way, that's what you really need in here. A yawn chair. And my mom's always got her breathing clients over there, and sometimes even their whispers can be loud."

"Nah, it ain't *your* folks," Herbert said. **"It's his."** Herbert pointed at Portico.

Portico could feel the frets come on, immediately. The inside stuff moving around. **Out of place. Piling on. Mixing up.**

"What you mean?" he asked, trying to play it cool.

"**They always arguing.** Wasn't always like this, but lately they've been really going for it."

Portico felt squirmy in his skin. He tried to explain the situation. "**It's weird right now.** We're in the middle of moving to two new apartments, and so, there's just a lot of talk about what stuff goes where."

"**Two new apartments?**" Herbert asked.

"Yeah. One upstairs and one downstairs," Portico explained. "**Gonna be pretty sweet.**"

"So . . . they getting **a   d i v o r c e ?**"

> (gulp)
> > (gulp)
> > > (gulp)

Divorce? Felt like it had an *X* in it. Like "divorxe," because of what it might mean. Portico's throat also felt like it had an *X* in it. Like something spiky caught in there. Or maybe something even more awkward, **like a question mark. Or questions.**

We not going to be a family **no more?**

My mum and dad not friends no more?

Is this gonna happen to me and Zola?

"I don't . . . I don't know," Portico muttered.

"Well, it definitely sounds like it," Herbert said. "They sound like my parents sounded before my father left." He pointed to a picture taped to the wall. It was of Mrs. Singletary the mum and a man who wasn't the Super. Must've been Herbert's father, Mr. Singletary the Dad.

"But my father ain't leaving. Just getting another apartment downstairs."

"Yeah, well, my father said he'd be around, too," Herbert said.

"When's the last time you seen him?" Zola asked.

Herbert just shrugged.

"But maybe the old rubbish man will stick around, y'know?" Herbert said, but this time it didn't feel like as much of an insult. "He's cool. Seen him giving Mr. Mister some new shoes yesterday. Velcro. No lie, your mom's cool too. There was this one time when she saved me from Romello Mann. He was trying to convince me that a tattoo would go good with my earring and that he knew how to do it. Said he learned in Alabama."

But Portico couldn't hear any of it. Portico couldn't hear much of anything but the pipes of the boiler room clanging in his ear, and . . .

Whose apartment am I supposed to live in? (Clang!)

Should I eat breakfast with mum and dinner with Dad? Lunch . . . in the stairwell? (Clang!)

Is this the real meaning of an APARTment? (Clang!)

Yo, watch this.

Zola said suddenly, desperately trying to break the tension. She jumped up and grabbed one of the pipes and did, I don't know, five thousand pull-ups. Portico knew she was doing it to distract him, and it was working, but even the distraction was distracted by sounds coming through the wall. Herbert shook his head. And even though Portico already knew what was going on, he put his ear to the wall.

OUCH, THE SOFA?

"Come on, the sofa has to be mine. It's *my* mother who sits on it all day long!" Portico heard his father say through the wall. It was muffled, but clear enough.

Portico frowned.

"What is it now?" Zola asked.

"The sofa," Portico replied.

"You know, they remind me of that episode of *Super Space Warriors*, when Mater and Pater get hit with that sonic boom," said Herbert.

"Episode 100. One of my favorites," said Zola.

"Mine too," said Herbert.

"Remember when the boom came, it knocked out their hearing for a while? So they couldn't understand what each other were saying, even though they were saying the same thing."

"Protect the sun," said Zola.

"Yep, and because they always mad at each other, they wouldn't even look at each other to see if they could read each other's lips. They just sat there trying to convince each other to do the right thing," said Herbert.

"**And did nothing,**" said Zola.

"And the Irators blew up their secret lab! **And it was—**"

"**AN EXPLOSION OF GREAT MAGNITUDE!**"they both howled.

But Portico was silent. **Sad.**

"**Yeah, I'm really sorry, man, but they remind me of that episode,**" Herbert repeated, this time putting his hand on Portico's shoulder.

And instead of becoming Stuntboy and rushing to save his parents from doing their own stunts, from hurting themselves, Portico stayed put. He had tried almost everything. **All his stunts.** The Zamarama Zigzag, the Potato Bug, the Pancake, the Untied Glide, and the Didn't Even See You Standing There at least six times. Maybe seven. But none of them seemed to be working. So instead of busting in, Portico simply shrugged at Zola and Herbert who, in this moment, revealed his secret identity as Herbert Singletary the Not So Bad After All. Then Portico jumped up and grabbed one of the pipes and knew *immediately* that was a bad idea. Because he hadn't turned into Stuntboy. Which means he was just plain ol' Portico. Which means no superhero arms. But Zola and Herbert helped him pull himself up anyway.

Episode 9

TWO FOR TWO

Roll Credits.
   Cue music.

Do any of y'all play the harmonica? No? The kazoo? Ah, we have a kazoo player? That'll do.

Let's do the song. But . . . through the kazoo, please.

And a one,
      and a two,
         and a . . .

WeLLLlllLcoMe to STUNtboyYYyy in the MeaNNnnNnTIme!

OOF

This is Portico Reeves.
This guy, right here.
HIM.

And I'm sure you can tell just
by looking at him that he's
having some anxiety.

That's because on
the 204th day of his
best best friendship
with Zola Brawner,
which also happened
to be his first day of
his kinda friendship
with Herbert the
Not So Bad After All,
he found out (or realized)
his parents were getting
divorced.

HOW TO FIND OUT YOUR PARENTS
ARE GETTING DIVORCED

1. Hang out in a boiler room with Herbert Singletary.

2. Say this to them:

Y'all getting divorced?

3. Listen for any of these word combinations (think of it like cracking a code):

"Our relationship"
"We love you"
"Things change"
"That won't change"
"These things happen"

"Not your fault"

PORTICO'S PARENTS SAID THEM ALL

On the **205th day** of his best best friendship with Zola, and his second day of his kinda friendship with Herbert, came the first day of endship for his parents. Or at least the first day they decided to just say all the words about it. **To Portico. Over breakfast.**

Like divorce. Well, they didn't actually say "divorce." Instead they said:

"**We're . . . separating.**" (Add that to the earlier list.)

And that was a fact! **They'd been separating EVERYTHING!** Fighting and fighting and fighting and fighting over who gets what. Not just the musical chair, the empty picture frame, the family portrait on the plate, the old clock, the coffee table, and the television, but also an ugly lamp, an even uglier lampshade, the left side of the bed (yes, only the left side), a wooden spoon, and even screamed and steamed over the tea kettle that screamed and steamed for them. And their apartment,

236

4D, piece by piece, turned into two giant piles of stuff, like junk monsters stacked to the ceiling. They covered the place in scary shadows and turned the apartment into an abandoned planet. Even the living room became a room with no ... living.

And just when Portico thought divorce could get no worse ... **it got worse.** Because the last thing to fight over was ... him.

Portico was sipping his orange juice, trying to swallow his feelings, when his mum said, **"Son, our apartment upstairs is pretty much ready. You're going to love it,** you'll see."

Portico's father choked on a chunk of scrambled egg.

"Pass me another waffle, please," said Gran Gran.

"He has a new apartment downstairs, too, you know," Mr. Reeves said. Then, turning to Portico, continued. "Your room is huge."

Portico liked the sound of that.

"Pass me another waffle, will ya?" Again, from Gran Gran.

"It's even bigger upstairs," his mother said.

Portico liked the sound of that, too.

"Another. Waffle. Please!"

Portico didn't like the sound of this part:

"YOU CAN PICK WHICH

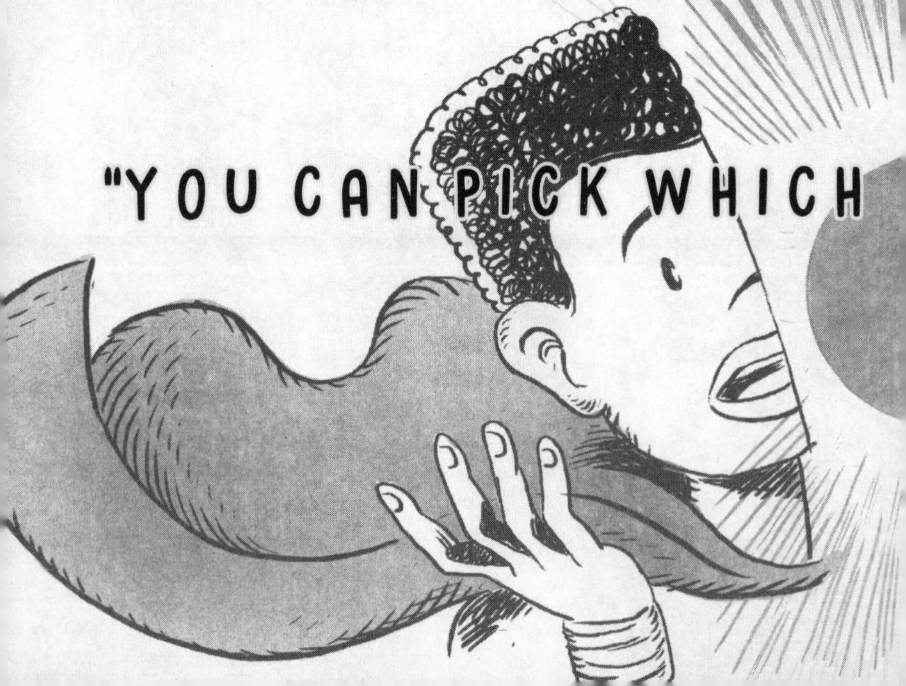

Because it sent his imagination twisting, and the inside-mixup started happening. **Frets. Like . . . *FRET FRETS!*** Suddenly, he could feel an itch on the top of his head. But this was a new feeling. So he went to scratch it, and it turned out not to be an itch at all. It was a hole. A tiny buttonhole in the top of his head that, when he scratched, opened and spread more and more and more, until it stretched down his forehead, between his eyes, right down the middle of his face and chest until **he was completely split in half.**

One hand.
One foot.
One eye.
One ear.

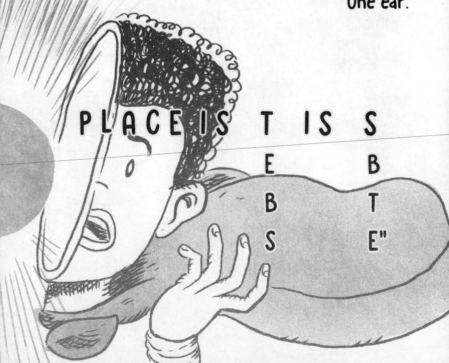

PLACE IS T IS S
E   B
B   T
S   E"

HALF AND HALF

The two halves of himself loved each other, but knew they now had to move in different directions. One went upstairs to his new home on the fifth floor. There, he recognized some of the things from his old apartment, but not every thing. There was a better view, but he couldn't really see all of it because he only had one eye. There was the old coffee table, his storm shelter, but there was no sofa. He did sit on the old fold-up chair, but couldn't keep his balance with only half a body. But he kept trying, because this was his new home.

His other half had gone downstairs to his new home with his father. It was nice there too. Not as much of a view, but that didn't bother him because he was closer to the front door of the building, which was nice since he only had one leg. The old clock was there, and the sofa, which he couldn't get comfy on. He loved the kitchen, but had a hard time eating without his other hand. Also, it was tricky swallowing without half his face, without half his taste tunnel. Weird.

Upstairs Portico went to check on Zola, but when he got to the door, she didn't recognize him. They'd been best best friends for 205 days, and she couldn't tell it was him. Portico tried to convince her, but he was having a tough time speaking, and well, he looked . . . different.

"It's me . . . Portico. I . . . promise."

"No, it's not," Zola said. "If you're Portico, what you call your anxiety?"

He concentrated so he could get the word out right, with his half mouth. **"Frets,"** he said.

"I use my superpowers!"

"What's your superhero name?" Zola zipped.

"Stuntboy!"

"Hmmm." Zola was still skeptical, even though Upstairs Portico was giving all the right

Okay, well, how do you get rid of them?

answers. "Then show me one of your stunts. The Zamarama Zigzag."

Portico tried to do it, but couldn't. Because he didn't have his other half. All zig but no zag. Which equaled a zoom into the wall.

His other half, Downstairs Portico, had gone looking for Herbert Singletary the Not So Bad After All. He wanted to tell him all about his new downstairs apartment. But before Portico got to the front door of the building, he saw Mr. Mister wearing his new Velcro shoes.

"Nice shoes, Mr. Mister," Portico said.

How you doing, young man?

"Young man" is what he called people he didn't know.

"It's me, Portico."

"And it's me, Fire Hydrant."

"I don't know what you talking about."

"And I don't know who you are."

"But I'm . . ." Portico decided not to try to convince him.
Mr. Mister only knew him as a whole boy, not as a separated

one. *Dang.* But hopefully Herbert, the kid who'd had his eye on him every day for years, would recognize him.

Portico spotted Herbert at the bench, sitting with a few of his other friends.

"Yo, Herbert," Portico called. Herbert turned around, but was looking at him with unsure in his eyes.
"It's me, Portico."

"You not Portico."

"I am too."

"Then tell me what I used to call you all the time."

Sheesh. There were so many names to choose from, but there was one he said the most.

"Snortico."

Normally, Herbert would've snorted at his own silly joke. I mean, he ALWAYS laughed at that. But suddenly, it didn't seem to be as funny to him.

"That was an easy one," he said. "Let me think of a harder test." Herbert thought for a moment. **"What is—"**

But Portico interrupted him and rattled off a bunch of things only he would know.

"You live with the Super but hide on the fourth floor in a boiler room because you still mad about your parents splitting up and your mum getting married again and you act tough but really you just want to watch *Super Space Warriors* and pretend to be a supervillain called the Boiler even though in your heart you wanna be a superhero like me but we're still trying to figure out your name and superpower and Zola suggested—"

"Okay, OKAY!" Herbert said, trying to get Portico to quiet his voice so the other weenagers wouldn't hear. "It's you." Herbert reached out to give Portico a five, but missed because Portico's left hand wasn't there. "But . . . you *different*. I mean, it's fine, but"—Herbert whispered low low—"can you still do your stunts?"

Portico tried to do a Floppity-Flip over the bench. Bad idea. Without his other half, it came out like a Flippity-Flop, which, take it from me, is *not* the same and *never* pretty.

Herbert's friends all started laughing, but as soon as Herbert gave them a double dose of the mean eyebrows, the laughing stopped.

"You okay?" Herbert asked, helping Downstairs Portico up.

"Yeah . . . no . . . I don't know."

"You okay?" Zola asked, helping Upstairs Portico up.

"Yeah . . . no . . . I don't know."

Suddenly, Downstairs Portico started moving backward. Back away from Herbert, who followed him. Back into the building. Back down the hall to the stairwell. Up the stairs to the fourth floor. Down the hall to apartment 4D, where Upstairs Portico (and Zola) were waiting at the door for him.

"We'll be out here if you need us," Zola and Hebert said as both halves of Portico backed through the door, sat back down where his mother and father were still arguing, and the two parts of himself glued themselves back together.

Oh, and Gran Gran had taken the whole plate of waffles.

THE FINAL WORD AND TWO FRIGHTS

"You can pick which place is best!" Portico's parents repeated, not even noticing what Portico was going through. Not even noticing that he'd been squirming in his skin, because the inside-mixup was the most mixed up it had ever been. And that all his insides ended up upside down. At least they felt that way.

Oh no. Not now, Portico thought. *Not . . . nowww.* There was no time for frets. Because not only had his parents not noticed

that he was freakin' out, not noticed the tears in Portico's
eyes, they also hadn't noticed the meow-cries from A New
Name Every Day.

But Portico heard them. Meows coming from somewhere.
But he didn't know where. So he got up.

He stood in front of the piles of things from his life, now
all in the wrong place. Stacked up, scary. Wobbly and weird.

With his frets. His parents still arguing.

And there was his cat, all whiskers and whiny, sitting on the head of one of the junk giants. On one of the frets on the *outside* of Portico's body, which had become . . . **frights**.

"Portico . . ." his father said, finally realizing Portico had gotten up. And was crying. "Portico, I . . . we . . . I'm so sorry." But there was no time for that now. Portico was trying to figure out how to save A New Name Every Day from these inside-mixup mess monsters.

"Son, do you hear us?" his mother asked. "Come . . . sit down. Let's try to talk about how you're feeling. Is it the frets?" But what they didn't know was that Portico had done something he tried to never do. Something that goes against the code of superheroes.

He'd become Stuntboy right in front of his parents.

TRASH

They'd been too busy bickering to tell he'd supered up, so luckily, his cover wasn't blown. But there was something he hadn't noticed before, something about himself, **a secret superpower: as Stuntboy**—*whenever* he became Stuntboy—Portico felt no frets.

No. Frets.
At all.

But in that moment, he noticed.
He noticed BIG-TIME.

"Baby, you hear me?" his mother asked again.
But Stuntboy couldn't hear a thing but the meow.

COMMERCIAL BREAK: This commercial is brought to you by

HOW TO TELL YOUR CAT IS SCARED

1. If it meows, it's fine.

2. If it me-owwwwwws, it's annoyed. With you.

3. If it meeeeeeeeee-ows, it's a scaredy-cat. (Check.)

Now back to your regularly scheduled program.

Stuntboy was afraid his cat would try to save itself and waste one of its lives, and because he'd had A New Name Every Day for so long, Stuntboy wasn't sure how many lives it had left. So, he did the only thing he could think of. The only thing he could do.

THE PLASTER BLASTER,
which he renamed in this moment, FRIGHT FIGHTER.

Portico took a step back.

Then . . . **took off!**

He leapt onto one mixed-up pile, and
using his foot, sprung off
from it, catapulting himself
into the other pile, where
he grabbed the cat and slammed
back down onto the floor
with a *thump-da-dump!*

"What in heaven's name
are you doing?!"
his mother yelled.

"Why on
Earth would
you do that?!"
his father followed.

But Portico'd saved
the day. **Again.**
Or at least saved the cat.

And as Portico got up and backed away from the frights—all the small things his parents had been fighting over—

he watched them wobble

and wobble

and wobble

No...

Oh, please...

and . . .

w o b b l e.

Gran Gran grinned. The cat did too.

And Stuntboy—

no-fret Portico Reeves—waiting for

AN EXPLOSION OF GREAT MAGNITUDE,

took a deep breath in.

And blew it out.

REINTRODUCING THE ONE AND ONLY...

THIS IS STUNTBOY. He used to be the greatest super-hero you've never ever heard of. But now you've heard of him. Because I can't keep secrets. Well, guess what? **There's one more secret to tell.**

Actually, **it's really a secret secret,** but I'm gonna let the cat out the bag.

You know how every superhero has a superhero trainer?

Someone who teaches them how to use their powers?

Well, where do you think Stuntboy learned all *his* stunts?

Stuntboy in the Meantime

Shhhhhhhhhhhhhhhhhhhhhhhhhhhhhhhhhhhhhhhhhhhhhhh . . .

To be continued . . .

Here are some of Raúl's sketches . . . I mean, practice stunts!

PORTICO PUNCH!

Kick!

ALWAYS DOUBLECHECK ING TO SEE IF FEET ARE STILL THERE.

MANY COLORS RAINBOW LACES FLOURESCENT LEATHER. EACH HAS SPECIAL SIGNIFICANCE TO HIM

MANY SPARE SHOELACES SLUNG OVER SHOULDER.

FEET WRAPPED IN LACES

Acknowledgments

JASON:
So many people to thank. Like, Caitlyn and Elena and Raúl and all the artsy-fartsy people who worked on this book and all the fartsy-artsy people who've read it.

And to my mother and father (miss ya, Pop!), who taught me the greatest stunt in the history of the world: love.

And that one, kids (and older kids, ahem), you can definitely try at home.

RAÚL:
To Jason's collaborative spirit. It was a thrill working on this book with you. To my father Raúl (Yuño) Gonzalez for teaching me how to observe people around me to find what makes them special. It has been helpful as I illustrate books filled with interesting characters.

JASON REYNOLDS is a #1 *New York Times* bestselling author, a Newbery Award Honoree, a Printz Award Honoree, a two-time National Book Award finalist, a Kirkus Prize winner, a two-time Walter Dean Myers Award winner, an NAACP Image Award winner, and the recipient of multiple Coretta Scott King Book Award Honors. He's also the 2020-2021 National Ambassador for Young People's Literature. His many books include *All American Boys* (cowritten with Brendan Kiely), *When I Was the Greatest*, *The Boy in the Black Suit*, *Stamped* (cowritten with Ibram X. Kendi), *As Brave as You*, *For Every One*, the Track series (*Ghost*, *Patina*, *Sunny*, and *Lu*), *Look Both Ways*, and *Long Way Down*, which received a Newbery Honor, a Printz Honor, and a Coretta Scott King Book Award Honor. He lives in Washington, DC. You can find his ramblings at JasonWritesBooks.com.

RAÚL THE THIRD is the three-time Pura Belpré Award-winning author-illustrator of *¡Vamos! Let's Go Eat* and *¡Vamos! Let's Go to the Market*, and the illustrator of *Lowriders to the Center of the Earth*, written by Cathy Camper. He is currently working on spin-off titles from the World of ¡Vamos!, which include El Toro and Friends, and Coco Rocho books. He lives in Boston. Visit him at RaultheThird.com.

ELAINE BAY was born and raised in El Paso, TX, and has been collaborating with Raúl the Third since the 90s. She has worked as a colorist on SpongeBob comics as well as the award-winning *¡Vamos! Let's Go to the Market* and *¡Vamos! Let's Go Eat*. She is currently working on more World of ¡Vamos! titles, and as a color consultant on the ¡Vamos! television adaptation. She is a master printmaker and performance artist making her home in Boston, MA, with Raúl the Third and their son Raúl the Fourth.